THE ORIGINS OF HEARTBREAK

LAKESIDE HOSPITAL SERIES, BOOK #1

CARA MALONE

ONE

Megan Callahan stood nervously on the side of a small stage at the front of an ornately decorated church, waiting for her name to be called. It was late September and she was standing in line with a hundred and fifty other people, all waiting to receive their white coats as they began their second year of medical school.

She had spent the morning going through all of the technical details of starting a new school year — figuring out her class schedule and purchasing her textbooks in the college store — and it had all seemed pretty anti-climactic. She'd been working toward becoming a doctor for as long as she could remember, and this felt like nothing more than a new semester at the same school she'd been attending for the past five years.

She'd already completed her first year of medical school, and now she was known as an M2 — one more year of classes and then she would finally be doing the hospital rotations that she'd been waiting so long for. It felt so far away still, and yet with a set of spotlights beating down on the stage and making Megan's brow moist, the significance of the white coat ceremony felt more real than ever.

She was two people away from the front of the line now, and very soon she would be walking across the stage. One of her professors would be putting a white coat on her shoulders, and by the end of this year she would be one step closer to becoming a real doctor, seeing patients and holding lives in her hands. Megan was doing her best to pretend she wasn't having a small panic attack about that, particularly because the student standing directly behind her—Ivy Chan—was an alpha dog through and through and she'd love any opportunity to observe weakness in Megan.

They had met in line at the bookstore on their very first day of medical school, and Megan made the mistake of trying to talk to her once she noticed that they were buying a lot of the same books.

"Are you a first-year med student, too?" Megan had asked.

"No, I'm just a really dumb third year," she said with a roll of her eyes. "Looks like someone's going to have trouble with evidence-based practice."

Megan had opened her mouth to rebut, meaning to throw something out about her biology degree and how Northwestern had given her a solid understanding of the scientific method, thank you very much, but then the line moved forward and the girl marched away with her books. Megan had hoped that in a class of a hundred and fifty, their paths wouldn't have to intersect again, but of course the universe couldn't be that kind. Ivy had been a constant thorn in her side ever since.

"Megan Callahan."

Hearing her name called into a microphone made Megan's heart give a little jump in her chest, and she ascended the stairs onto the stage. One of her favorite professors, Dr. Morrow, was holding out a white coat for her. As Megan turned around to put her arms through the sleeves, she scanned the audience, looking for her parents. They were out there, along with her younger brother, but the bright lights obscured them.

The twirling process of putting on the coat was a little awkward and disorienting, and then Dr. Morrow was guiding Megan on her way across the stage to shake hands with the dean.

"Ivy Chan," the announcer called. Megan spared a glance backward and saw Ivy slipping gracefully into her coat.

Megan exited on the other side of the stage and went back to her place in the pews to wait for the rest of the class to finish getting their coats. Her nerves had dissipated the moment she felt the coat settling on her shoulders, and she couldn't wait to go back to her apartment and check it out in the mirror, complete with a stethoscope looped around her neck. It was worth every bit of the last five years of work, staying up late and studying after everyone else went to sleep, burning the midnight oil to keep up on social events at her undergraduate sorority and still get her work done. There was still a lot of hard work left to do, but a little bit of recognition and a crisp white coat was nice, too.

After the ceremony finally drew to a close with Megan's class reciting the Declaration of Geneva (*I solemnly pledge to consecrate my life to the service of humanity...*), they were all released to greet their parents and take them over to the student union for a reception. Megan found her family lingering outside of the doors of the church, and her folks immediately made a huge deal out of the coat, hugging her and inspecting the material. Her mother straightened her collar while Megan blushed and tried to lead them across the courtyard.

"You look like such a grown woman," her mother said, her eyes tearful from the ceremony.

"You look like a marshmallow," Megan's teenaged brother, Finn, said.

"A marshmallow that has the power to save—or end—your life," Megan shot back, but he paid no attention to her reply. He was looking longingly toward the student union, where a lot of people were headed.

"There's food at this thing, right?" he asked.

Megan watched Ivy come out of the church alone and march across the courtyard with the same pompous posture she'd had when she walked across the stage. She wondered if Ivy had anyone in the audience watching her, but it was impossible to feel too sorry for her when she wore that perpetual scowl on her face that said she had the world's most uncomfortable stick up her butt. Megan stopped watching her and said, "Yeah, let's go—I'm starving."

The four of them headed over to the reception, where there were hors d'oeuvres galore, from finger sandwiches to mini quiches to a chocolate fountain surrounded by fresh fruit. Finn split off from the rest of the family instantly, making a bee line for the dessert table, and Megan picked up three champagne glasses for herself and her parents.

Before she'd even taken a sip, though, her roommate, Chloe, came bounding over, practically skipping across the room and throwing her arm around Megan's shoulder.

"Hi Mr. and Mrs. Callahan," she exclaimed, then turned to Megan and did a little impromptu fashion show with her white jacket, twirling around and then bumping her shoulder against Megan's. "How excited are you? I don't think I'm ever going to take my white coat off."

"I'll probably take mine off to go to the grocery store and stuff like that," Megan said with a small laugh. Chloe was the most enthusiastic, bubbly person Megan had ever met. Half the time, she felt compelled to put her hands on Chloe's shoulders just to keep her from floating away, and the other half of the time she wanted to install a zipper on her mouth.

"Oh, I won't," Chloe said with a half-serious grin. "I want *everyone* to know I'm a doctor."

Then she threw her arms around Megan again, giving her a quick peck on the cheek, and dashed off to mingle with more people. Megan watched Chloe go over to Ivy, who was stacking a plate high with finger sandwiches, and Chloe greeted her with the same enthusiastic energy.

Megan always expected Ivy to sprout quills like a porcupine whenever people approached her, but for some reason she didn't have the same prickly response to bubbly Chloe that she had to everyone else.

My colleagues will be my sisters and brothers, Megan thought, remembering another line from the Declaration of Geneva. Then she thought, *This is medical school.*

TWO

Alex McHenry felt like the only person in the room who was on the verge of vomiting from nerves. It was the last day of September and her first day of class, along with about twenty other people enrolled in the Emergency Medical Technology program, and the technical school was pretty different from the University of Illinois where she studied last year. At least she was pretty sure what to expect from a first day.

There were introductions to be made, and syllabi to be read, and they'd probably get an overview of the EMT program and a reading assignment or two. It shouldn't be a big deal for Alex, but she was nervous. By the end of this program, she would be responsible for saving people's lives.

The girl sitting at the desk beside her was the only other student who seemed even remotely stirred by this fact—she was actually shaking a little bit. Most of the other people in the room, by contrast, just looked bored.

The instructor hadn't arrived yet, so Alex leaned toward the shaky girl and said in a confidential tone, "They're probably going to have us do some ice breakers. Do you want to get a head start?"

"Huh?" the girl asked.

"I'm Alex," she said. She didn't get nervous often anymore, and she thought if she could channel her nerves into putting this girl at ease, then she might feel better, too. Alex extended her hand and the girl took it. "What's your name?"

"Sarah," she said, then withdrew her clammy hand.

"What are you in for?" Alex asked.

"What?" Sarah asked, furrowing her brow at Alex's question, but before she could explain that it was a joke, a man in a button-down, short-sleeved shirt and a thin tie walked to the front of the room and started writing on the board, snapping Sarah's attention away from Alex.

He wrote his name in thick letters—Mr. Zachary Chase—and then turned around to address the class. He had a stack of papers to hand out—just as Alex anticipated—and as he passed them around the room, she focused on the routine of syllabus reading and became less nervous.

"Welcome to Evanston Community College, and to the EMT training program," the instructor said with a smile. "I'm Zach Chase and I'll be your tour guide. Please keep your arms and legs inside the car at all times."

Alex gave a little snort at this, along with a few other laughs from the class, but mainly everyone was just staring at

Mr. Chase as he made his way back to the front of the room. Alex hoped that this was nothing more than first-day jitters, otherwise the next few months were going to be a drag.

The papers turned out to be a program overview rather than a syllabus. In order to obtain an EMT-Basic certification, Mr. Chase said, they would all be completing one semester's worth of classes, including anatomy and physiology, basic life support, and hands-on experience. They would all become CPR-certified in that time, and at the end of the program they should be ready to take a licensing exam and begin working in the field. Alex skimmed through the packet as he talked, reading off the list of skills she would need to obtain in the next three months.

Cardiopulmonary resuscitation. Assessment of emergency care requirements. Lifting, moving, and transporting patients. Recognizing the nature and severity of a patient's condition.

It was a lot to learn in such a short time, and a weighty responsibility. Alex looked around the room and wondered why everyone else looked bored by this instead of anxious. Last year she'd been learning how to teach art class, and the year before that she was in high school, responsible for no one and nothing. It was only recently that she decided to make this quantum shift into medicine.

She was having second thoughts.

"Okay, that's enough of listening to me ramble," Mr. Chase said. "We're going to get up and get the blood flowing, get to know each other a little bit. Everybody, circle the wagons."

There was much noise and chairs scraping along the linoleum floors as he directed everyone to rearrange their desks into a semi-circle. Then he retrieved a stack of index cards from his desk and stood in the center of the circle.

Alex ended up next to Sarah again, and no sooner had her butt hit the chair than Mr. Chase said, "Up and at 'em. I told you guys we're getting the blood flowing."

Everyone stood up, and then he went to the first desk in the semi-circle, laying down an index card with a name written on it.

"Dan Armstrong, pop a squat," Mr. Chase said, pointing at the desk. "I'm seating you all alphabetically so that it'll be easier for me to remember your names, and on the back of your name tag I wrote down a question. When you get to your seat, you're going to answer the question for the class."

Dan turned out to be a tall guy who looked like he was in his forties, with muscular arms and wide shoulders. He'd have no problem with lifting, moving, and transporting patients. He sat down and looked at the question on the back of his index card.

"Why did you enroll in EMT classes?" he read, and then without hesitation, he answered for the class, "I've been an orderly at Lakeside Hospital for fifteen years, and I realized pretty early on that I would never be able to move up without an education. Life got in the way, but

I'm here now to better myself for my career and for my kids."

"Thanks for sharing, Dan," Mr. Chase said.

He slapped another index card down on the desk next to Dan's and called another name, and then another, as more and more people found their new seats. Most of the questions were in a similar vein—digging into people's motivations and goals for enrolling in the program—and Alex learned that there were not many people in the class who were like her, without any previous medical training. A lot of them were older, returning to school for a second or even third career, and the majority of them were already working as nurse's aides or caregivers of some sort.

It was beginning to make sense to Alex why she felt like the only nervous one in the bunch.

Then Mr. Chase called her name.

"Alexandria McHenry," he said, and she winced. He noticed it and asked, "Problem?"

"I never go by my full name," she said. "I prefer Alex."

"Alright," Mr. Chase said, completely nonplussed as he scribbled the corrected name onto her index card and then put it down on her desk. "Plant yourself, Alex."

She sat down, then looked at her question. *What will make you a good EMT?* She wanted to laugh—after half the class talked about their medical experience and the loved ones that they cared for at home, she was no longer sure that she was in the right place.

But everyone was looking at her and waiting, so she

read the question out loud and then said, "I've been told that I'm good in a crisis. I'm calm on the outside even when I'm panicking inside. I make level-headed decisions most of the time, and people tell me I'm comforting."

"Thank you, Alex," Mr. Chase said, then flipped the next index card down on the desk beside her.

THREE

A few weeks into her second year of medical school, when October was under way and the smell of burning leaves could be found whenever she went outside, Megan went with her class to the County Medical Examiner's Office to observe an autopsy. They were in the middle of a pathology module in class and they had been discussing the causes of disease, so Dr. Morrow arranged for a clinical experience that would tie into his lectures.

Megan had been in a cadaver lab for her human anatomy courses last year, but this was one of her first forays into seeing an actual patient, regardless of whether that person had a pulse. Chloe was so excited for it that she had barely slept the previous night, and this morning Megan found her sitting at the dining table with her pathology textbooks and *Gray's Anatomy*, squeezing in a little last-minute studying while she waited for her oatmeal to warm up in the microwave.

"What do you think the cause of death is going to be?" she had asked as Megan shuffled toward the coffee maker.

"Mmpfhh," Megan groaned. She would have been more excited about the field trip if she hadn't woken up with a pounding migraine that morning, and her only concern at that point had been to caffeinate as a means of counteracting it.

"Maybe it'll be a murder," Chloe said, her eyes lighting up. "Like something on *CSI*."

"Doubtful," Megan had said.

"Hey, a girl can dream," Chloe answered, irritated that Megan wasn't in the mood to play along with her. She flipped her blonde hair over her shoulder and went into her bedroom to get dressed while Megan propped her hands against the kitchen counter and waited for the coffee to percolate, her head throbbing behind her eyes.

When it was time to go, Chloe drove and Megan sat in the passenger seat, using the visor mirror to try to make herself presentable. Her red hair was frizzy and she couldn't be bothered with makeup while her head felt like it was in a vice, but at least her white coat was crisply ironed after Chloe noticed her pain and took pity on her. There were a *few* benefits to living with a perpetually cheerful, nurturing type.

Megan's head was feeling a little better by the time they arrived at the Medical Examiner's Office, thanks to a large cup of coffee and a couple of Excedrin. She and Chloe went inside and a receptionist greeted them cheerfully, almost as if they were there for a hair appointment, not to look at the inside of a human body.

The lobby was clean and new—and a tad too bright—and through a nearby door, Megan could see a row of cubicles just like any other office building. The first thing that seemed a little out of place was the security keypad on a door at the back of the lobby, which the receptionist carefully shielded while she punched in her code. The door swung open on an automatic track and the building transitioned abruptly from office to laboratory. There was a long hall with doors along both sides, labeled with words like *Toxicology* and *Histology*.

"The autopsy suite is the last door on the right," the receptionist said, waving Megan and Chloe into the hall, and then she headed back to her desk.

They found the right place, a large room with a loading bay at one end and a couple of steel autopsy tables at the other. The majority of their class was already present and accounted for, and Ivy was standing in the only place Megan would expect of her. She was right in front of one of the steel tables, a legal pad in hand, taking notes on every aspect of the autopsy suite that she could see.

"Ready to test out your bedside manner?" Megan quipped to Ivy as she and Chloe found places near the end of the table. "This is probably the only place where it would be appropriate."

"Wow, Megan," Ivy said, turning her nose up as she looked at her. "So nice of you to arrive looking professional and groomed. I think there's a spare body bag around here somewhere if you need it."

"Be nice to her, she has a migraine," Chloe chastised, slipping her arm around Megan's shoulder. She managed to say it without a hint of irritation in her voice. As far as Megan could tell from their interactions in class, Chloe was the only person in the entire program whose head Ivy hadn't bitten off at least once in the last year. It was kind of remarkable.

Ivy turned back to her notes and Chloe asked Megan, "Are you feeling okay? Do you need another Excedrin? Some water? A snack?"

Megan waved her off, thinking that it must be pretty hard to be mean to someone who literally did not kill spiders. In the last year, Megan had come home on three separate occasions to find glasses from the kitchen upended on various surfaces in the apartment, spiders trapped under each of them alongside a note in Chloe's bubbly handwriting asking her to *pretty please* take them outside.

Megan was always tempted to just kill them because it was easier—they lived on the third floor so carrying a hairy, gross spider down three flights of stairs was no picnic—but in the end, she always rescued the stupid things like Chloe wanted. She shrugged herself out of Chloe's embrace and turned her attention back to the room around her.

"Look at that enterotome," Ivy was saying, pointing with her pen at an instrument tray full of sterilized tools.

Megan rolled her eyes at her while Chloe leaned over

and inspected the instrument. It was nothing more than a pair of scissors with a specially curved end to prevent unintentional cuts, but Ivy was showing off, making sure everyone knew she'd done her research, and the Medical Examiner wasn't even there yet.

The door to the suite opened again, and this time another large group entered. None of the newcomers were wearing white coats—instead they all wore blue polo shirts with *Evanston Community College* embroidered over their pockets—and Megan noticed that a few of them looked sort of pale and skittish.

"Paramedic students," Chloe said, whispering it to Megan like it was a secret. "I hear they bring them to an autopsy before they go into the field so that if they're going to pass out or vomit, they do it here instead of during a real case."

"Megan might beat them to it," Ivy said, but she at least had the presence of mind to murmur this latest insult—she'd meant it to be harmful to Megan, not to the EMT students.

"I'm fine," Megan said with a wave of irritation. She wondered just how long she would have to put up with Ivy's dominant, aggressive posturing. Last year she'd harbored the hope that once exam time came around and Megan had a chance to trounce her, Ivy would lay off, but the fact that Megan was ranked higher in the class by the end of their first year only served to spur Ivy's insults on.

Megan watched the EMTs come into the room. They were looking all around and noticing the mortuary refrigerators along one wall. A few of them seemed to be actively avoiding them, looking anywhere but the refrigerators and the autopsy table, and Megan wondered which one of them would be the first to hit the floor when the autopsy got started.

A couple of them were chattering nervously and Megan listened in on their conversation because it was either that or continue to listen to Ivy's impromptu lesson on autopsy instrumentation.

"We're not, like, *all* going to end up here, are we?" one of them, a chubby blonde, asked. She was staring at the ambulance bay on the far wall as if she were looking into her own morbid future.

"No," said the girl standing next to her. "The Medical Examiner doesn't handle natural deaths, so most people don't get autopsied when they die."

Megan found herself drawn into their conversation. The blonde looked uncomfortable in this sterile, slightly ominous setting, but the second girl had an air of stoicism about her that was intriguing to Megan.

She didn't seem to fit with the rest of the group, and she most certainly didn't look like the type of person that made a successful paramedic. She was tall, thin but not too skinny, with long, chestnut-colored hair, a button nose, and a youthful face. Megan guessed her to be eighteen or nineteen, not far out of high school. She didn't look like the type of person who could handle the responsibilities of being a paramedic—Megan wondered how she'd ever lift a fallen patient, or ride in the back of an ambulance without her small frame being thrown around at every turn. Then again, a lot of people surprised Megan ever since she started medical school—she never would have dreamed that someone as tiny and cute as Ivy could contain so much ire.

Realizing that she'd been staring at the paramedic and her friend for far too long, and that their conversation had moved on from autopsies to study sessions, Megan turned away and tuned back in to Ivy's mini-lecture.

"A lot of people don't realize that not everything you find in an operating room, or an autopsy room as the case may be, is actually manufactured as a surgical instrument," she was saying. "Kitchen shears, for instance, when sterilized properly..."

Megan's headache had turned from sharp and nauseating to dull and throbbing but still persistent, and the room was beginning to heat up with all of the people standing around her. She felt herself growing impatient and wondering where the Medical Examiner was. She just wanted to get this field trip over with so she could go home and crawl back into bed until her headache was nothing but a distant memory.

FOUR

The week leading up to the field trip to the Medical Examiner's Office had been characterized by a lot of nervous energy in Alex's class. Watching an autopsy was something that everyone in the paramedic program at Evanston Community College did—a rite of passage and also a bit of preparation for the worst type of emergency they would be responding to on the job.

Most of Alex's classmates spent the week wondering what their reaction to seeing a dead body would be. Poor Sarah looked white as a sheet that morning when they met in the Medical Examiner's Office parking lot.

"I want to help *living* people," she said. "I don't understand how this is relevant or necessary."

"People die sometimes," Alex said.

For all the nerves she felt over the prospect of working as a paramedic, this particular day didn't bother Alex at all. This was not the first time that Alex would see a dead body. She wasn't worried about passing out, or vomiting, or being unable to handle the sight. The only thing Alex was worried about was the possibility that she might burst into tears and be unable to stop.

Just over a year ago, her father died and she still hadn't cried about it.

The Medical Examiner wasn't there yet by the time the rest of her class—along with Mr. Chase—arrived and they all went into the autopsy suite, and Alex passed the time by walking slowly around the space, examining the laboratory. She reassured Sarah that not everyone ends up here, and that was true. Thankfully, Alex's father had never laid on an autopsy table or else Alex didn't think she could stand being there.

It was a heart attack, one of the most clear-cut natural deaths a person could have. He was in the kitchen dicing vegetables for dinner and she was sitting on the couch in the living room, using her laptop to register for her sophomore classes at the University of Illinois. Her mom wasn't home from work yet and she was calling back and forth to her dad, planning what to get for her mom's birthday. Then she heard a loud metallic clatter as her father dropped the knife he was using.

"Shit," he muttered, and she half-rose out of her seat to check on him, asking what happened, but he said, "I don't know. Butter fingers, I guess."

He didn't sound concerned. Alex sat back down, trying to focus on her schedule again, but an unsettled feeling was growing in her stomach. Something wasn't right. A minute later she heard something else fall, much heavier this time, and she flew into the kitchen to find her father on the floor, slumped against the cabinets.

"I'm having a dizzy spell," he said, looking at her with confusion. He had his hand on his chest, and Alex felt her pulse beginning to race. She froze in the doorway, trying to make sense of the scene. He was dizzy—*what do you do for dizziness?* She thought about telling him to put his head between his knees, but then his eyelids fluttered shut and that was what finally pushed her into action again. She grabbed his phone off the counter and dialed 911, dropping to her knees beside him while she waited impatiently for the operator to tell her what to do.

The operator talked her through a rudimentary form of CPR, and eventually the sirens of an ambulance blotted out all the other sounds in Alex's world. Paramedics rushed into the kitchen and took over, and Alex just kept thinking that dinner would be ruined if she didn't remember to put the meat back in the refrigerator before they went to the hospital. It couldn't sit on the counter or they would have nothing to eat later.

No one ate that meal, though. The world came crashing to a halt that night for Alex and her mother, and the vegetables her father was chopping sat on the counter for days before Alex got up the courage to throw them away.

Then for a long time life stood still, until one day last month Alex enrolled in EMT school. The paramedics that responded to her father's emergency were so fast and so good at their jobs, and they even found the time to be comforting to Alex. She never wanted to feel that helpless again. She wanted to be like those paramedics instead.

She led Sarah over to the autopsy table, standing behind a row of what must be medical students, all in white coats. Alex steeled herself, determined to get through this field trip without breaking down. She was a blank slate ready to learn from this observation and completely divorce it from her real-life experiences.

WHEN THE MEDICAL EXAMINER finally arrived, trailed by two assistants in surgical scrubs, the conversation in the room trailed off. The Medical Examiner stood near the front of the room and addressed everyone, introducing himself as Dr. Markovich, but hardly anyone was actually looking at him. Behind him, his assistants were opening one of the mortuary refrigerators, and all eyes—Alex's included—were glued to them.

The door yielded a few wisps of condensation, nothing like the dramatic cloud of chilled air that forensic television shows trained Alex to expect, and then the assistants pulled out a long steel rack on top of which lay the body. Alex felt Sarah slip her hand into her palm, squeezing it tight, and one of the assistants retrieved a gurney that had been pushed up against a nearby wall.

"The decedent has arrived with us by way of the Emergency Room," Dr. Markovich was saying. "He is a fifty-four-year-old male who was found in the midst of a grand mal seizure in his office two days ago. By the time the paramedics arrived, he had become unresponsive and despite efforts to resuscitate, he was dead shortly after arrival in the ER. There was no past history of seizures."

Alex watched as the two assistants lifted the body —*the decedent*—onto the gurney and she had a sudden, overwhelming urge to raise her hand.

Dr. Markovich looked rather perturbed by her interruption, but he nodded at her. "Yes?"

"What was his name?" Alex asked, glancing at Mr. Chase to gauge how out of line this question was. She didn't think she could watch an autopsy without knowing anything about this person except his age and the circumstances surrounding his death. Judging by the critical looks she was getting from some of the medical students, the medically relevant information the Medical Examiner provided was all they needed.

Dr. Markovich had to look down at the tablet in his hand, consulting an electronic chart, but he did answer her question.

"Paul Goulding," he said, and then without waiting for any further remarks from the audience, he went on. "Since *Mr. Goulding* was an otherwise healthy man and the cause of his seizure and subsequent death is unknown, we are now going to see what the body can tell us about the cause of death."

The two assistants wheeled the gurney over to the table where everyone was gathered, and the difference between the two groups of observers became obvious. Everyone in a white coat leaned in, fighting for a place closest to the table, and everyone in an Evanston Community College polo took a step back.

"What do you think it is?" one of the medical students, a pretty Asian girl, whispered to her classmates. "I'm thinking status epilepticus."

Status what now? Alex thought, wondering just how far outside her comfort zone she had put herself. The other medical students threw in their two cents with other potential diagnoses while Alex's class just watched in silence.

Sarah squeezed her hand again as the assistants put the body down on the table. Alex wasn't too easy to rattle, but she did jump a little at the way they did it with such efficiency. She couldn't blame the assistants—they'd probably done this so many times that they didn't even have to think about it anymore, and with the nature of their work it was almost certainly necessary to create a little space between themselves and the *decedents*. Still, it was so... mechanical.

Paul Goulding, she thought as they took the gurney away and Dr. Markovich stepped up to the table.

"If anyone is feeling queasy at any point during the autopsy, there's a bench just outside the ambulance bay where you can get some fresh air. *Please* resist the urge to vomit in the autopsy suite," he cautioned with a tired expression, as if he was reciting this message for the hundredth time. "There's always one."

Alex let go of Sarah's hand and inched closer to the table. She was *not* going to be the one that broke down. She straightened her posture and steeled her resolve, looking over the shoulder of a redheaded medical student and trying to avoid the curly hair that was flying in a million different directions from her messy ponytail. It was clear that Alex and the rest of her class wouldn't get any better view of the table than this, since all the medical students were standing practically shoulder to shoulder in the front row, looking more like kids on Christmas than people about to see an autopsy.

Dr. Markovich picked up a scalpel from the instrument tray and began, narrating his actions for the benefit of the students and so that one of his assistants could type his findings into the tablet.

"A coworker of the decedent told paramedics that he reported feeling sick earlier in the week," Dr. Markovich said as he worked. "Nausea, fever, that sort of thing. She thought nothing of it because it's flu season, but of course any symptoms may become clues so we must keep them in mind as we conduct our investigation."

After a few minutes, during which she noted gratefully that no tears were threatening to rise in her throat, Alex looked around the table to take stock of her fellow students' reactions. Mr. Chase was standing toward the back of the room, doing the same thing. He smiled briefly at her, and continued to scan the room. Everyone seemed just fine, and even Sarah was watching with wide eyes.

For her part, Alex felt like she was watching the autopsy with a removed sort of feeling, as if from the perspective of a second person floating a few feet above her. There was no sorrow, or revulsion, or anything at all. It felt just like watching the paramedics push her father's gurney into the back of the ambulance. It felt like nothing, because she couldn't connect that sight to her own reality.

On the day that her father passed, it was as if a switch had been flipped in Alex's brain, turning off her emotions to protect her from the pain of losing him. Some part of her had chosen to become numb, and when the shock started to wear off, she wasn't ready to let those emotions come crashing back to her so she let her therapist prescribe anti-depressants that kept that comfortable numbness going as long as she needed.

After a year of being numb, Alex should have known that nothing could break through the hard shell she'd formed around herself—not even watching an autopsy. Still, she'd come to the Medical Examiner's Office today with a lingering fear that if anything could pierce her unfeeling shell, this would be it.

She was just beginning to wonder what today would have felt like *without* anti-depressants when a tuft of red hair tickled her nose. The med student in front of her had swayed backward and Alex stepped away, rubbing her nose as the girl straightened up. Then suddenly she was coming at Alex again, falling this time. Alex had just enough warning to put out her arms and turn her face away so the back of the girl's head wouldn't smash into Alex's nose on the way down.

FIVE

Megan opened her eyes to see the tall, pretty paramedic from earlier looking down at her. For just a moment, she noticed the stunning, steel gray of her eyes.

Then Megan looked past the girl and saw that everyone in the room was looking at her—looking *down* at her. She was on the floor, in the paramedic's lap to be exact. Suddenly her headache was a complete non-entity, and the flush that had been rising into her cheeks for the past few minutes was gone as well. She was in a cold sweat, anxious and embarrassed at having fainted.

She scrambled away from the girl, standing up and catching the eye of Dr. Markovich in the process. His scalpel was paused mid-air and he had a look of mild annoyance on his face because she hadn't shown him the courtesy of fainting outside as he'd requested.

Chloe caught her arm as she stood up and Megan tried to shake her off. She felt embarrassed enough without her over-protective roommate propping her up like an invalid.

"Are you okay? Do you need to go outside?" Chloe asked. "Do you need water?"

"Jeez, Chlo," Megan muttered, overwhelmed and irritated. "Enough questions. I'm fine."

The room was just too hot, and there were too many people crowding around her at the table. The surgical lights above it were beating down on her and she had begun to feel light-headed from taking that Excedrin on an empty stomach. It was nothing more than an ill-advised diet and a hot room that had made her pass out, but everyone was still looking at her and she felt the urge to explain it to them. She did *not* want to be that idiot who couldn't handle a little blood and guts—especially not that *medical student* idiot. If anyone was going to pass out, it should have been one of the EMTs.

"I had a migraine earlier," she murmured, but it sounded like a lie or an excuse even to her own ears. They all thought she was a wimp—she could see it in their eyes.

"Amateur," Ivy said under her breath. The look she was giving Megan matched the one Dr. Markovich had shot her as she was getting up from the floor, and Megan knew she was never going to live this one down. Ivy was a formidable opponent as it was, and now she'd have all the ammunition she needed to heckle Megan from now until graduation.

"Are you sure you don't want to get some fresh air?"

Chloe asked, attempting to brush Megan's hair off her damp temples. "You look peaked."

Most of the eyes in the room were still fixed on her, including the poor girl she'd fallen on, who had made it back to her feet and was looking at her with more concern than Megan would have preferred. Everyone looked like they'd be more comfortable if she just left the room.

"Yeah, okay," Megan said, and when Chloe tried to follow her, she added, "I'll be fine. You stay."

"But–"

"Seriously," Megan said, a slight irritation edging into her voice. Chloe always meant well, but her nurturing instinct tended toward smothering and Megan just wanted to get away from everyone who was looking at her as if she'd just done the most unfortunate thing in the world. Chloe looked genuinely disappointed that she couldn't be of use, and Megan turned away before she could try again to follow her.

"As I said earlier, there's always one," she heard Dr. Markovich say to the group with a self-satisfied smirk. "Are we ready to continue?"

There was a door beside the ambulance bay and Megan slipped as quietly as possible through it. Outside, she found the bench Dr. Markovich had mentioned, with a full ash can sitting beside it. She guessed that its existence wasn't solely to provide relief for medical students who couldn't handle their migraine medications—the employees must use it for smoke breaks.

She sat down and took a deep breath, letting the cool

autumn air fill her lungs and appreciating the breeze on her warm cheeks. She put her head back against the brick wall of the building and exhaled at length, letting the tension out of her body and allowing her mind to go to a place where she hadn't just made an ass of herself in front of her entire class and her mortal enemy.

It really did make her feel better to be in the fresh air, and when she opened her eyes, she saw a basketball hoop affixed to the wall above the loading bay. She let out a small laugh at the unexpected sight, then took another long, deep breath. The door opened again, and Megan was surprised to see the poor EMT she'd fallen on coming outside.

"Are you okay?" they asked each other in unison, and Megan smiled.

"Yeah," she said. "I woke up with a migraine and I didn't eat anything for breakfast. Caffeine and Excedrin on an empty stomach, plus hot lights and a crowded room, apparently equals fainting spell. Rookie mistake."

"I'm glad you're feeling better now," the girl said as she reached into her backpack and pulled out a bottle of water, moving closer to Megan and extending it to her. "Here. It's sealed."

"Oh, thanks," Megan said, taking it with a small laugh. "I was definitely worried you had the ulterior motive of coming out here to give me a water bottle full of backwash, but since it's sealed I'll take it."

The girl yanked the bottle away just as Megan reached for it. "If you're going to be an asshole then I don't want to help you after all."

"Is that how you're going to decide how you'll treat your future patients?" Megan asked, amused and intrigued by this girl who could dish it out as well as she could take Megan's sarcasm. "Because I have to tell you, people who are in pain tend to be assholes."

"Don't I know it," the girl said, sitting down on the bench. As she handed the bottle to Megan, she said, "I'm Alex, by the way."

"Megan," she answered, unscrewing the cap and taking a quick drink. "So I'm pretty sure everyone in my class thinks I'm a wimp now."

"I don't know about that," Alex said, smiling at her. There were those steely eyes again, stunning. She added, "But Dr. Markovich definitely thinks so."

"Shut up," Megan said with a wry smile, taking another sip.

Her head was beginning to clear for the first time since she woke up, and the flush that had risen into her cheeks was being chased away by the cool breeze. She knew she should go back inside—the longer she stayed out here, the worse it would look to her professor and the more relentless Ivy's teasing would be. But another part of her thought that the damage was already done and she selfishly wanted to stay here and talk to Alex a little more. She'd been working so hard, didn't she deserve a little break spent with a pretty girl?

"So how's *your* head?" Megan asked. "I didn't hit you on the way down, did I?"

"No," Alex said. "I have cat-like reflexes and I jumped out of the way just in time. You actually hit the ground like a bowling ball. I just scooped you up in my arms after the fact so you'd think I was the type of person who lets strangers collapse on them."

"And what type of person is that?" Megan asked. "Unlucky?"

"I wouldn't say that," Alex said.

Then an ambulance pulled into the driveway, letting out a single *wop* of the siren to notify the people inside the autopsy suite of its arrival. It startled Megan out of the moment and she looked away from Alex, drinking a little more water and wondering what had gotten into her. This morning she thought she was going to vomit from the pain in her head, then she was dying to get home and sleep off her headache, and now she was lingering out here and staring into the eyes of a complete stranger. It had been a hell of a day and it wasn't even lunchtime yet.

They watched as the ambulance bay's overhead door was opened from inside and a couple of paramedics jumped out of the ambulance to greet the Medical Examiner's assistant on the other side. They passed him a chart to sign, then they pulled a stretcher out of the back of the ambulance, a body bag laying on top of it.

Alex turned her face toward Megan, looking away from the ambulance, and then she tried to cover the motion by digging into her backpack.

"You okay?" Megan asked.

"Yeah," Alex said, but she was not at all convincing.

She pulled a pencil out of her bag and showed it to Megan as if it were proof that she found what she was looking for. Megan glanced behind her as the paramedics wheeled the stretcher into the autopsy suite and Alex twirled the pencil through her fingers a few times and then threaded it behind her ear. The paramedics returned, this time with an empty stretcher, and pushed it back into the ambulance.

"It's safe now," Megan said quietly.

"Safe for what?" Alex asked, but she seemed visibly relieved to watch the door to the ambulance bay being lowered.

The ambulance drove past them and paused at the street, waiting for its turn to merge into traffic, and Megan asked, "Are you sure you want to be a paramedic?"

"Yeah," Alex said.

"And you know that might be you someday, right?" Megan asked, nodding at the ambulance.

"Mm hmm," Alex said, pressing her lips tightly together. She looked like she was really struggling to keep the stony expression that she put on when the ambulance arrived. Megan didn't get a chance to question her further, though. The door opened again and the whole group of students poured out.

Shit, she thought, realizing that she must have missed the remainder of the autopsy. She shouldn't have been so slow to recover and go back inside.

The EMTs came outside first and Alex stood up when the blonde she'd been talking to earlier approached and asked if she was ready to leave. Alex gave Megan a quick wave, then rejoined her group.

Then Ivy came out, and of course her eyes zeroed in on Megan right away. She curled her lip and said as she passed her, "Not everyone who's book smart has what it takes to be a doctor. Think about that before you sink another hundred grand into a career you can't handle."

SIX

"I'm sorry you're not feeling well," Chloe crooned to Megan on their way back to the apartment. She hadn't stopped chattering since she burst out of the Medical Examiner's Office, full of energy as always and excited about the learning experience the autopsy had provided.

"I'm fine," Megan said, and she could hear herself getting a little short with Chloe, but it was at least the third time she'd told her this. The truth was that if she *did* still have a migraine, Chloe's incessant talk would be making it worse. She was a sweet girl and she meant well, but Megan missed Alex's calming presence already.

"Well," Chloe continued, "if it makes you feel any better, your fainting spell wasn't the most memorable part of the autopsy."

"I very much doubt that," Megan said. Ivy's parting words were still ringing in her ears, and even though Megan knew Ivy was just trying to get into her head, she still wished that she hadn't given her a reason to think she didn't have what it took to be a good doctor.

"Things got eventful after you left," Chloe said. "Dr. Markovich examined the brain and it turns out the patient had *meningitis*."

"Seriously?" Megan asked, perking up.

"Yes," Chloe said enthusiastically, making Megan a little anxious about her ability to drive and talk about medicine at the same time. "It was so cool. Dr. Markovich retracted the dura membrane and everybody immediately gasped. It was so overrun with bacteria it was like looking at a zombie brain."

"What did it look like?" Megan asked. It really had been stupid to waste her time outside, entertaining the thought of flirting with some girl she'd probably never see again, when she could have been gaining a valuable medical experience. That was what she was paying fifty thousand dollars a year for, as Ivy had so compassionately pointed out.

"It had hemorrhaged and the actual brain tissue had this greenish tinge to it because of the bacteria. Dr. Markovich said it was a once-in-a-lifetime find because usually they make the diagnosis in the hospital and they would have done the autopsy there to avoid contamination," Chloe said, and Megan groaned.

She'd *definitely* missed something important and she was starting to get angry with herself. Her whole life had been about exceling in medical school for the past year, or at the very least staying ahead of Ivy, and here she was getting senselessly distracted by a pretty face. She wondered if she could blame that lapse of judgment on the migraine, too.

Chloe reached across the center console to pat Megan's hand and added, "It was actually pretty gruesome. Maybe it's a good thing that you went outside."

"For the hundredth time, I wasn't sick," Megan said. "I had a migraine."

"Well in any case," Chloe went on, graciously ignoring Megan's irritability, "they don't normally allow audiences in the autopsy suite when the patient had a communicable disease. We really shouldn't have been there, but since they didn't know about the meningitis until they opened him up, we all have to get tested and take antibiotics just to be safe."

"Wow," Megan said. "Is it really that big of a deal?"

Chloe shrugged and said, "Well, that guy died pretty quick, so I guess it's better to be overly precautious."

"Paul Goulding," Megan said, remembering the name that Dr. Markovich had provided during his overview of the case—the name Alex had wanted to know.

"What?"

"Nothing," Megan said. "Was there anything else important that I missed?"

"Not really," Chloe said. "Ivy asked about a million meningitis questions, and Dr. Markovich seemed pretty upset about the whole situation—both the unexpected meningitis and Ivy's relentless questions. Most of the EMTs seemed pretty freaked out, and Dr. Morrow said we'll have a lecture on meningitis sometime this week to talk more about the disease."

"She told me I didn't have what it takes to be a doctor," Megan huffed.

"Dr. Morrow?" Chloe asked, aghast.

"No," Megan answered. "She Who Must Not Be Named."

"Oh," Chloe said with a nervous laugh. She hated to talk negatively about anyone, even when the person in question was clearly the devil in a white coat. "Well, she didn't know you're not feeling well. Do you want to go over to the hospital now and get it out of the way?"

They were already most of the way home, but Lakeside wasn't far away, either.

"Does it have to be today?" Megan asked. She was exhausted in the wake of her migraine and she still desperately wanted to climb into bed and sleep for a couple of hours before their afternoon lecture.

"They said that sooner was better, but it can wait until tomorrow if necessary," Chloe said. "I want to get it out of the way so I'm going today. We could go together."

She looked over at Megan with those big blue eyes and optimism in her voice. It was that kind of look that always kept Megan guessing—she could never quite tell if Chloe had a crush on her, or if she just looked at everyone that way. Megan hated to disappoint her, but there was no way she was going to spend the rest of the afternoon in a hospital lab.

"There's probably going to be a huge line," Megan said. "I bet everyone else from our class *and* the EMT class will be there."

Including Alex. The possibility of seeing her again

intrigued Megan, but if she was being honest, that was another good reason to put off the task until tomorrow. She'd already missed one important milestone in her medical education because she couldn't pull herself away from that girl—she wasn't going to let herself get further entangled with her. It would be best if she just never saw Alex again.

So Megan decided to play into Chloe's delusion that she was deathly ill and asked, "Can you please just drop me off at the apartment on your way so I can get some rest? I'll go in the morning."

"Oh," Chloe said, looking disappointed. "Well, if you want, I can stay with you. I could make you some soup, or get you a cold compress—"

"It's a headache, not the plague," Megan said. "I'll be fine."

"Okay," Chloe answered, and Megan felt guilty for not letting her be helpful.

She and Chloe had been living together for a little over a year, after Megan posted an ad on the university's housing website the summer before med school began, and in that time she learned that being helpful and nurturing were two of Chloe's favorite things. She was always going out of her way to do Megan little favors and help her out, and it felt cruel to be so unreceptive. On the other hand, Megan had also discovered that Chloe could be a real pest sometimes with all that heavy-handed nurturing, and she really just wanted a few hours to herself.

"Thank you, though," she said to soften the blow of her refusal. "I appreciate it."

When Chloe pulled up in front of the apartment building, Megan opened her door to get out and Chloe stopped her by asking, "That EMT student, the one that caught you–"

"Alex. What about her?"

Chloe narrowed her eyes at Megan for a moment, studying her, then asked in her usual chipper tone, "What did she follow you outside for?"

"She didn't follow me," Megan found herself lying, not entirely sure why she was doing it. "She just needed some air, same as me."

SEVEN

Alex headed straight home after the autopsy was over, driving with the radio off—something she almost never did. Ever since she first started driving, taking lessons from her endlessly patient father instead of her anxious mother, she always had music playing in the background to keep her company. Today she wanted the silence, though. She wanted to commit every aspect of the past few hours—and her unexpected encounter with Megan—to memory. She wanted to sit with those feelings, something she hadn't wanted for a long time.

The autopsy hadn't been what she expected, and it hadn't elicited the uprising of emotion that she'd been afraid of. Alex found it sad to watch Paul Goulding being moved around the autopsy suite, examined and analyzed as if he had ceased being a person and was now a puzzle to be solved. But it didn't break her.

What almost got to her was the ambulance pulling into the driveway and the way Megan had said, "It's safe now," like she could see right through Alex. *How could she read her like that when Alex couldn't even read her own muted emotions most of the time?* She pushed the thought away and took the slowest route, trying to think of things she could do besides going home.

Her mother would certainly have a dozen questions for her about her field trip, and there wasn't a lot Alex could do to avoid them. She had no other classes today, and she'd already gone to the grocery store over the weekend. She'd done a thorough job of pushing away all of her old friends after her father's funeral, so she didn't even have someone she could call to meet her for a cup of coffee. She thought about Sarah, but they were class friends, not *going for coffee* friends. Alex would have to go home eventually, and she might as well get her mother's comments out of the way. She'd been very vocal all week about how she didn't think Alex should go to the Medical Examiner's Office, saying over and over that she could probably get a note from her therapist to skip it, but Alex told her it was part of the curriculum and she was going.

Her mother was sitting in the living room when Alex got home. She would have been surprised to find her anywhere else—Dana McHenry had not moved voluntarily from the couch since the day their lives stood still last year.

"Well?" she said as soon as Alex poked her head into the room.

She was wearing the same saggy black sweatpants she'd been in yesterday, and she had her laptop on the couch cushion beside her, a sure sign that she'd just finished ordering yet another useless item from the Home Shopping Network.

"Well, what?"

"Was it awful? Are you okay?"

"I'm fine, ma," Alex said, and for the most part, it was true. She wasn't about to tell her mother about the panic that had risen in her throat when she saw the ambulance doors opening, or how that sight had dragged her instantly back to the moment when she had to watch the same scene in reverse, her father being loaded up and taken away in an ambulance whose sirens remained off as it pulled onto the street. She just said, "It was fine."

"Okay," her mother said in an unconvinced tone. Then she turned her attention back to the television, where a too-chipper sales woman was demonstrating the durability of a silicone baking mat.

Alex wondered if it was what her mother had just finished ordering. If it was, she could pretty much guarantee that it would never get any use in the McHenry house. Her mother had taken a leave of absence from her department store job last fall, and that leave had turned into a permanent state of motionlessness on the couch. Now she spent her days slowly feeding the money from Alex's dad's life insurance policy into the Home Shopping Network.

Alex couldn't be too critical of her mother because she'd spent the last year in a similar fashion, and in some ways her mom had a right to the skepticism she showed about Alex's field trip, but suddenly Alex felt the need to

44

defend herself—gently. She ventured, "You know, you're the one who encouraged me to go back to school. That's all I'm doing."

"I encouraged you to go back to the program you started at the university," her mother said. "I wanted you to finish your bachelor's degree, not enroll in this paramedic program. Alex, honey, it's a morbid fixation and it's not what I want for you."

Alex let out a little laugh before she could stop herself. They'd had this discussion several times before, and she'd never been able to properly explain to her mother how pointless her previous studies had become to her after what she'd gone through.

"It's not morbid. Paramedics save lives," Alex said, and then as she turned to go to her room, she called over her shoulder, "You should get changed and take a shower, ma. I'll make us lunch soon."

She always had to sound casual and off-handed about her mother's hygiene, trying not to give her the impression that she was judging her, but if Alex didn't say anything then her mom would stay in those same baggy sweatpants until they became threadbare and stretched out.

With a sigh, Alex headed down the hall to her bedroom at the back of the house. It was a teenager's bedroom, something she hadn't cared to redecorate since she moved away to live in the dorms her freshman year of college, and which she didn't have the energy to deal with now. The walls were a bubblegum shade of pink, the curtains were obnoxiously purple and glittery, and her bedspread was vividly floral. Every time she walked into the room she thought that something with muted tones and minimalist vibes would fit her new mood more than the cluttered femininity that it actually reflected, but she never got any further than thinking it.

Alex dropped her backpack on the floor beside her desk and turned on her computer so that she could play some music. In the last few months, she'd graduated from the angry vocals of bands like Mindless Self Indulgence and Nine Inch Nails to the lullaby melancholy of Coldplay and Twenty One Pilots, and she wasn't quite sure if this was a good change or a bad one.

Turning the music up just enough to drown out the cheerful, consumerist drone of the Home Shopping Network coming from the living room, Alex sat down in a worn old armchair by the window. It had once held pride of place in her father's makeshift hangout spot in the garage, and it was the only thing Alex had changed about her room since moving back home. She watched cars go lazily down the street outside and let her mind drift back to Megan.

She had been interesting in a way that Alex hadn't found anyone to be in a long time. There was nothing in particular that made Alex follow Megan outside, except maybe for the vulnerability she saw in her eyes when they'd been on the floor together. Megan seemed just like all the other cocky doctors-to-be until that moment, and she'd even given Alex a hard time after she went outside to check on her, but there was something soft beneath that coarse exterior.

Alex could relate to that.

She leaned her head back against the chair and closed her eyes, allowing herself to imagine what it would have been like to work up the courage to kiss Megan while they were sitting alone on that bench.

Alex had been out of the dating game for a while—if she'd ever truly been in it—and she could have been imagining the tension between them just because Megan was so stunningly pretty, with those emerald eyes and that fiery hair... and those curves. In the five minutes or so that they were alone together, Alex couldn't even decide if Megan was gay, let alone interested in her. But she could dream.

Alex opened her eyes.

There was no point in indulging this fantasy. It had been a nice diversion from the emotional strain of the autopsy, but her path would almost certainly never intersect with Megan's again.

Alex heaved herself up from the comfort of the overstuffed chair and went into the small bathroom connected to her bedroom. She opened the medicine cabinet and grabbed a prescription bottle, flipping the top off with her thumb like she'd done a few hundred times already. The little blue pill that she shook into her palm had become a symbol of comfort to her over the past year. They kept her most unmanageable feelings of grief at bay and allowed her to exist in a state of comfortable numbness, observing but not participating in the world around her. Her mother had the Home Shopping Network, and Alex had anti-depressants.

She shook the bottle and about ten pills rattled in it. She had a week and a half before she'd have to go back to the pharmacy and get another refill, but lately Alex was beginning to wonder if the pills were still helping more than they were getting in her way. Most of the time she liked being numb—it was like a secret weapon that the unfortunate folks who had to feel their emotions didn't have access to—but every once in a while, it got in the way.

Like today.

She wondered what it would have been like to sit on that bench next to a gorgeous woman without a persistent undercurrent of apathy running through her. Alex could say all the right things, and know on an intellectual level that she found Megan attractive and wanted to flirt with her, but Alex wasn't really *feeling* the chemistry between them in the way she wanted to.

Alex reached for a glass sitting next to the sink, using it to wash down her daily dose of numbness. When she got back to her room, she noticed that her phone was vibrating in her backpack. The music playing on her computer nearly drowned it out, but she managed to fish out her phone before she missed the call.

"Hello?"

"Hey, Alex," said Sarah. "You ran out of there so fast I didn't get a chance to talk to you."

"What's up?" Alex asked, a little confused. She'd see Sarah again the following day, and the only reason they'd even bothered to exchange numbers was to ask each other to take notes in case one of them couldn't make it to class.

"I wanted to make sure somebody told you about the antibiotics," Sarah said. "Did Mr. Chase talk to you?"

"No," Alex answered. "What antibiotics?"

Sarah explained the big excitement over the autopsy, the meningitis diagnosis, and the infectiousness of the disease. She told Alex that the whole class had to be tested and treated with a prophylactic course of antibiotics to prevent it from spreading further.

"That brain was so nasty," Sarah said, wrapping up her report. "I thought I was gonna puke."

"Well, I'm glad I didn't have to see it," Alex said. "Where are we supposed to go for the antibiotics?"

Sarah gave her the details and then Alex hung up to call Lakeside Hospital and schedule an appointment. Most of the class had already done so and the earliest they could fit her in was the following morning. Alex noted the location and time in her calendar, then opened her bedroom door to shout down the hall, "Hey, ma, can you fix your own lunch? I've got some studying to do."

"Yeah, that's fine," her mother called back, and Alex closed the door again. There was no reason to worry her over something with such a low probability—Alex hadn't even been in the room when Dr. Markovich autopsied the brain—but that didn't mean she wasn't going to take every precaution until she was immunized, and that included isolating herself for the night.

EIGHT

Megan woke up the following morning feeling much better than the previous day. The last lingering effects of her migraine had dissipated, and she'd gotten more sleep than she had on most nights since she began medical school. She was a little behind in her studying and her readings since she'd opted for a mid-day nap instead of studying like usual, but that was a small price to pay to be clear-headed once again.

The apartment was empty like it always was on Tuesday mornings, when Chloe had an early morning lab and Megan didn't have anything scheduled until noon. Ordinarily, she liked to idle in the silence of the apartment in those rare moments when she had it to herself. Living with Chloe was often like living with a Tasmanian devil, but it was nice to have someone to split the rent with.

Getting ready in a leisurely fashion wasn't in the cards today, though. Megan had an appointment at the hospital lab in one hour to be tested and treated for her meningitis exposure. She threw on a pair of jeans and a cozy sweater to keep her warm in the brisk fall air, then packed her bag with textbooks and headed out the door. She would take the bus to the hospital and use that time to do a little reading, then she'd walk from the hospital to campus and spent the rest of the morning catching up in the library before her classes began.

WHEN MEGAN ARRIVED at Lakeside Hospital, she was no further along with the chapters she should have been reading, but she was much more knowledgeable on the diagnosis and pathology of bacterial meningitis. When she reached into her bag to pull out a textbook on the bus, she'd found her phone first and her curiosity got the better of her—she wanted to know more about the disease that had taken out Paul Goulding so fast, and which she had a chance of contracting.

By the time she stepped off the bus, she knew that viral forms of the disease were much less deadly, and that the strain of bacterial meningitis Paul had could be lethal in as little as twenty-four hours. She learned that the most likely setting for contracting the disease was a high school or college campus where people lived in close contact with each other, thus heightening their exposure in the event of an outbreak. Megan had memorized all the common symptoms, which perfectly fit the overview that Dr. Markovich had given of Paul's case yesterday, and she read about the typical progression of the disease.

The bus dropped her closer to the Emergency Room doors than the main entrance of the hospital, and Megan could have walked down the sidewalk a little way and entered through a large lobby with helpful receptionists pointing her exactly where she needed to go, but she entered through the Emergency Room. She was becoming more and more intrigued by Paul's case, and she wondered if a quick trip through the place where he died might yield further insights.

Part of her expected to find that everyone in the ER was wearing surgical masks and had been immunized against the disease. She expected some kind of change in standard operating procedures indicating that something significant had happened there.

Instead, it looked like any other Emergency Room.

There were a lot of tired and unhappy-looking people sitting around in the waiting area, in various states of illness and injury. There was a nurse's station where people came and went constantly, answering phones, responding to codes, and checking in new arrivals. Patients who had been given priority by the triage nurses were laying in beds that were lined up against two walls, privacy screens pulled between each one, and a group of doctors and nurses were clustered around one of the beds at the end of the hall, resuscitating a patient while his monitors went crazy.

Megan was standing in the middle of the space, frozen about halfway to the nurse's station while she took everything in, when a pretty brunette in a long white coat stopped in front of her.

"You need help?" she asked, looking Megan briefly in the eyes as if to assess her mental state or the dilation of her pupils, then glancing back down at the tablet in her hands where she was hurriedly typing notes into an electronic chart.

"No," Megan said, amazed at the girl's speed. She wondered how long she'd been a doctor, and whether her velocity was a byproduct of working in the ER, or if she was always like this. "I'm just looking for the lab."

"Third floor. Go down the hall, turn right, elevator bank is on the left," the girl rattled off, then started to walk away.

"Wait," Megan called after her, and when the girl turned back she glanced at her badge. *Krys Stevens, M.D.* Megan figured that this multi-tasking wonder probably didn't have time for her, but the most she could do was tell her to get lost, so she decided to go for it. "Dr. Stevens, I'm a medical student and I was wondering if you remember a patient who was here earlier this week. I'm interested in the case."

Dr. Stevens looked mildly conflicted, glancing toward the nurse's station as if she had a million things to do, but she stayed and said, "There's only so much I can tell you without violating privacy laws, but if you make it quick and show me some identification, I'll tell you what I can."

Megan quickly dug her student ID card out of her wallet, showing it to Dr. Stevens as she explained, "I observed an autopsy at the Medical Examiner's Office yesterday and the patient had bacterial meningitis–"

"Yep, I definitely remember that," Dr. Stevens answered, cutting her off. "They called us yesterday and everyone that was on staff the day he was here had to start a round of antibiotics. Real pain in the butt and we fell behind for the rest of the night. Everybody was extra crabby because the wait times were so long."

"Was there anything remarkable about the case that you can recall?" Megan asked.

All the online literature reviews in the world couldn't make up for some good, old-fashioned primary research, and she wanted to hear from someone who had a hand in Paul Goulding's care before he became part of the Medical Examiner's domain. She wanted to know if there was a reason why the ER doctors hadn't identified his condition, and whether that was a common occurrence. How often did people trace a path from the Emergency Room to the autopsy suite without a clue about their cause of death?

"I can't really help you there," Dr. Stevens answered. "He was unresponsive upon arrival. We continued resuscitation attempts that the paramedics had initiated, but he died shortly thereafter. There really isn't anything more to report about that case."

"Oh," Megan said, disappointed, and she was just about to launch into a line of questions about how the Emergency Room was protecting its other patients against the disease when an ambulance pulled up outside and Dr. Stevens and a few others snapped into high alert.

"Gotta go," she said to Megan, already rushing toward the door. "Good luck with your research."

Megan stayed a little bit longer, watching as the sliding glass doors opened and the doctors and nurses flooded out to assess the incoming patient. Not wanting to be in the way, and aware of the fact that she'd been in the ER longer than she intended and was running the risk of being late for her appointment, Megan followed Dr. Stevens' directions to the elevators in the hallway.

She went up to the third floor and, after a few minutes of walking through the hall and reading the directories on the walls, she found the lab. She was just reaching for the door handle when it swung open, and the person who came out—nearly knocking her to the floor—was none other than Ivy.

Megan rolled her eyes—if anyone was going to send someone to the Emergency Room from inside the hospital, it would be Ivy.

"Excuse me," she said, stepping out of Ivy's way lest she sustain further injury. "I didn't realize the queen was coming through."

"I didn't mean to knock into you, Megan," Ivy responded with feigned sincerity. "Are you okay or do you need a bottle of water and a time out?"

"I'm fine now, and I was fine yesterday," Megan answered.

"Are you sure? I could call a nurse," she said, then winked and added, "or a paramedic."

"I'm sure," Megan answered, clenching her teeth. Ivy had a way of getting under her skin, and Megan was shocked that she'd made it this far into the program without giving in to the nearly constant desire to slug her. Instead, she decided to hit Ivy where she knew it would hurt the most. She said, "I was doing just fine when I finished last year three spots higher than you in the class, anyway. What's your rank, again?"

"We're only a third of the way through the program," Ivy growled at her. "We'll see who's on top at the end, when it counts."

She started to walk away, handing the victory for that little verbal spar to Megan, and rather than being a gracious winner, Megan couldn't help saying, "Eighth."

Ivy's shoulders visibly tightened at hearing her class rank—clearly it was a number she wasn't comfortable with—but she didn't turn around. She just kept walking toward the elevators, and Megan went into the lab. She would probably never convince Ivy that her fainting spell yesterday had been a complication of her migraine instead of a result of the autopsy, but at least she could hold onto this little victory for as long as she managed to stay ahead of Ivy in the class rank. It was her primary goal in life, at least for the time being.

She went into the lab and signed herself in, then sat down in the nearest empty chair. The room was pretty full for a Tuesday morning, about a dozen other people waiting for bloodwork, scans, and other tests, and their morale didn't seem much better than those waiting in the ER downstairs. Megan set down her backpack and pulled out a textbook, ready to use this time to cram in a little extra studying—it wasn't easy being fifth, and after running into Ivy, she was regretting the time she took yesterday to rest. But before she could dive into her textbook, Megan's eyes fell on the occupant of a chair on the other side of the room.

It was Alex, the EMT student who had caught her yesterday, and she was watching Megan's every move. A shiver went through her as she felt those steely eyes on her, and she looked away.

She was surprised to find her pulse was slightly elevated. There was no reason to believe that a medical student and a paramedic-in-training would cross paths again, at least not until Megan stared her rotations, so she didn't put much stock in the way she was drawn to Alex yesterday. But here she was, and Megan found herself entirely too excited by this serendipitous event.

She wanted to keep looking at Alex, really study the features of her face this time and see how much subtle flirtation she could accomplish before the lab technician called one of their names. She wanted to find out if the tension she felt yesterday had been real.

More than any of that, though, she wanted to get caught up on her reading so that she could continue to kick Ivy's butt in class that afternoon. She wanted to protect her rank and prove to Ivy and anyone else who might be doubting her that she had what it took to be a damn good doctor. She couldn't do that if she kept letting Alex distract her in crucial moments, and the way her body reacted when she was nearby was a warning sign that Alex could be dangerous if Megan were to indulge those desires.

She could tell that from all the way across the room.

She decided it would be best to pretend she didn't see Alex, or didn't recognize her. She pulled her textbook open in her lap and kept her head down, ready to study. She read the same sentence several times, though, and she just kept wondering what Alex was doing.

She didn't have to wait long to find out. In her peripheral vision, Megan saw Alex stand, pause for a moment as if uncertainty had just grabbed hold of her, and then she crossed the room.

Megan couldn't contain her curiosity any longer. She abandoned the ruse of the textbook and looked up. The waiting room was no more than fifteen feet across, but it feel like a runway as Megan watched Alex close the space between them, her hips swaying seductively from side to side, her eyes locked on Megan's in a way that made her heart beat faster.

When Alex got to her, she gave Megan a friendly smile and pointed to the seat next to her. "Can I join you?"

"Umm, yeah," Megan said, scooting her backpack out of the way and feeling irritated at the uncertainty in her own voice. She never reacted like this to girls—*she* made girls react like this to *her*.

NINE

Alex sat down in the thinly cushioned chair beside Megan, wondering if she was imposing on her. She hadn't really stopped thinking about Megan since their encounter the previous day, and when she spotted her across the waiting room it seemed like fate had brought them back together, but Megan had immediately pulled out a book and looked away.

Alex had already been sitting there for at least ten minutes because the lab was backed up from the morning rush, and she couldn't imagine spending another ten minutes sitting awkwardly across from a girl she thought she'd had a moment with yesterday. So she took a leap of faith, and decided to find out if that moment had been real.

"Are you feeling better today?" she asked.

"Yeah," Megan answered. "The migraine cleared up pretty quickly and I got a lot of sleep last night, but if I remember your side of the story correctly, then that was due to the concussion I sustained when you let me hit the floor."

"Sounds about right," Alex said with a laugh. She was relieved to see Megan sliding her textbook back into her bag. If she really didn't want to talk, then she would have ignored Alex and gone back to reading *The Pathologic Basis of Disease*. She nodded at the book as Megan zipped her backpack and said, "That looks like a real page turner. Are you sure *I'm* the cause of your sleepiness?"

"Maybe not," Megan conceded. "So who knew we missed the most eventful autopsy ever?"

"Yeah, it was crazy," Alex said. "I didn't find out about the meningitis until after I got home. A girl from my class called me, said it freaked her out. Apparently, it was pretty gruesome."

"I probably would have thought it was cool," Megan admitted with a smile. "But then again, I spent the bus ride over here researching everything I could find about the disease, so I might be coming at this from the perspective of a—"

"Nerd," Alex supplied with a grin, cutting her off.

"I was going to say doctor," Megan said with a thank-you-very-much air, but Alex could tell she was teasing. Flirting? "So your classmates are freaking out. How are you holding up?"

Alex shrugged. She honestly hadn't given the possibility of contracting meningitis too much consideration, aside from sequestering herself in her room last night to protect her mother. She wasn't worried about it, but then she wasn't worried about much these days. That was the best benefit of her anti-depressants, keeping her on an even keel whether it was warranted or not.

"It's probably that whole youthful immortality thing," she said with a shrug. "I really don't think it could happen to me."

"Meningitis?"

"Meningitis, death, all of it," she said, wondering if she'd gone too dark, too fast. She studied Megan, looking for her reaction and wondering if she should lighten the statement with a joke. She didn't have a lot of those in her repertoire lately, but she could try to muster one for a girl like Megan.

"No one's immune to getting hit by a bus," Megan pointed out, "but your odds of contracting meningitis from a deceased person whom you shared a room with for less than an hour *are* pretty low. I was reading up on the antibiotics we have to take and they're basically just a safeguard against the worst-case scenario. The patient died less than twenty-four hours after contracting the disease, so on the off chance that any of us have it, they can't waste time on diagnostics before they start giving us the treatment."

"Hurray for preventative medicine," Alex said. "What exactly *are* we doing here, by the way?"

"No one told you?"

"No, my friend was too busy telling me how close to puking she was to give me the details," Alex said. Then, giving Megan a side smile, she added, "Enlighten me."

It was meant to be a little bit flirtatious because there

was just something intriguing about Megan that begged Alex to get closer to her. She didn't think anyone would have the power to break through the haze of her little blue pills, but Megan made her want to try.

Alex studied her reaction closely, eager to know whether Megan would pick up on the tone of her voice and the way she was smiling at her, if she'd even be interested if she did pick it up, or if she'd just answer clinically.

"Well, what we're getting in the lab is a throat culture," Megan said, and although it was a technical answer, the fact that she turned her body sideways in the chair to address Alex, her knee brushing against Alex's thigh ever so slightly, wasn't lost on her.

"Ugh, a throat swab?" Alex asked. "I thought I was done with those when I got my tonsils out."

"They're awful, aren't they?" Megan commiserated. "My roommate wants to go into pediatrics, but I don't think I could handle gagging kids with cotton swabs all day."

Alex laughed, hoping that this banter was more than the friendly passing of time while they waited for their turn with the lab technician. Her flirting was pretty rusty and talking about throat cultures probably didn't count as seduction, but she thought that—unless she was reading the signs all wrong—Megan was interested in her. She kept her eyes locked on Alex as they talked, her lips parting periodically to show her perfect white teeth as she smiled.

"So that's it? They're going to jam a swab down my

THE ORIGINS OF HEARTBREAK

throat and then I get to go home and take antibiotics until they tell me I'm healthy?" Alex asked.

Megan said, "Yeah, that's about it. It could take up to twenty-four hours to get the culture results, and since the disease can move so fast we have to start the antibiotics immediately."

"Well, that sounds like a nail-biting good time," Alex said.

"It beats being dead," Megan answered with a smile.

"That's true," Alex said. "I hope they have a toy drawer."

Megan arched an eyebrow at Alex, and in that moment she simultaneously realized the unintentional innuendo in what she'd said, and saw intrigue in Megan's eyes. That answered the question of whether Megan played for her team, and it also sent a furious blush into Alex's cheeks.

"I mean like my doctor had when I was a kid," she said quickly, as Megan laughed good-naturedly at her embarrassment. "Cheap yo-yos and bouncy balls and stuff like that."

Before Megan could let her off the hook, the door to the treatment area opened and a guy with a clipboard stepped out and called, "Alexandria McHenry?"

Alex was only too eager to remove herself from that humiliating moment, so she stood up. She wondered if it would be too forward to give Megan her phone number right now, but the lab technician was looking rather impatiently at her, and she figured that the lab was so backed up Megan would likely still be waiting here by the time she finished her dreaded throat swab. By then, Alex might well have recovered from this moment and gotten the color out of her cheeks.

"Good luck in there," Megan said, and then she reached for her textbook again and Alex followed the technician.

He led Alex down a short hallway with small patient rooms on both sides. Reading from the chart, he said, "Ms. McHenry, can you confirm your date of birth for me?"

Alex told him, and he led her into the last treatment room. There was a small exam table in one corner, a cabinet across from it, and a chair for the technician to sit in. He remained standing and motioned Alex over to the exam table.

While Alex sat down on the crinkly paper, he asked, "And you're here as a result of the meningitis exposure, correct?"

"Yes," Alex answered, feeling a little anxious.

She really did hate throat swabs, and she remembered every single one from her childhood, thanks to bout after bout of strep throat. Her dad usually took her to the doctor's office because his job was salaried so it wasn't as big a deal for him to leave work as it was for her mom, and Alex used to squeeze his hand as hard as she could while she opened her mouth and waited for the doctor to gag her with the swab.

The anticipation was always the worst part, and today she had no hand to hold and no one to distract her. She watched the technician put on a pair of gloves and a surgical mask, then he took a long, flat package out of one of the drawers in the cabinet. He carefully removed the cotton swab and prepared the vial it would go into.

Alex decided to think about Megan. Anything was better than focusing all her attention on the torture instrument coming at her, and Megan was a very easy subject to latch onto. Alex couldn't remember the last time someone made her feel like Megan did, her cheeks burning, her pulse racing and her stomach doing flips. Just sitting beside her sent electricity through Alex's body, and she wondered what it would be like to actually touch her, to thread her fingers into Megan's or to kiss her.

Alex probably shouldn't be thinking about her like that. She knew almost nothing about Megan except that she was a medical student, she was clearly very smart, she was a knock-out, and she had—on at least one occasion in her life—had a migraine. Maybe that was enough, though, at least to take the next step and see what she was like outside of a clinical setting.

The technician swabbed Alex's throat, she gagged as expected, and then the dirty business was done and she was released with instructions to go straight down to the pharmacy, where an antibiotic prescription would be waiting for her.

MEGAN'S CHAIR was empty when Alex got back to the waiting room, and she stood there for a moment, wondering if it would be crazy to wait for her. She *thought* Megan seemed interested in her, but Alex had been swimming in a haze of numbness for so long that she didn't completely trust her instincts anymore. Maybe she'd misread the entire situation and Megan would be confused or displeased to come back from her throat swab and find Alex waiting for her.

On the other hand, Alex didn't have anywhere to be for another hour and a half and she thought the chances of accidentally running into Megan a third time were pretty slim. It was now or never, so she took a seat and waited for her, trying not to look too eager.

She pulled a compact mirror out of her bag and looked at herself, hoping that her cheeks weren't too red after the throat swab. Megan may have fainted on her, but Alex didn't want to ask Megan out looking like she'd just finished dry heaving. Her cheeks were a little flushed and her hair was a bit wild, so she combed it as best she could with her fingers and then put the mirror away.

Megan came out a minute or two later, and with a racing heart Alex stood up to meet her.

"Aww, you waited for me," Megan said, clearly trying not to sound too charmed, and Alex grinned. Now *that* was the desired effect.

"I just wanted to give you something," Alex said, feeling the heat rising back into her cheeks as she reached into her backpack. "I mean, just in case we survive this meningitis outbreak."

"What is it?" Megan asked, tilting her head to the side and smiling as she studied Alex's flustered state.

"My number," Alex said, taking Megan's hand quickly before she lost her nerve and writing it across the back of her hand with the first writing implement she found—a blue highlighter.

Megan looked at it as Alex capped the marker, making sure she could read all the digits, and then because she'd run completely out of bravery, Alex gave Megan an awkward little nod and said, "Anyway, I'll see you around."

Then she turned and headed for the door, feeling torn between elation and embarrassment. She had no idea what the smile on Megan's face meant—it could have been anything from flattery to sympathy, and Alex just had to get out of there before she found out it was pity.

TEN

Megan smirked as she watched Alex walk toward the door. She didn't want to give in to this distraction from her studies, but if Alex was going to hand-deliver herself, then Megan couldn't resist her any more. She pulled her cell phone out of her pocket and quickly punched in Alex's number, and she could hear the vibration of Alex's phone in her backpack.

Alex stopped with one hand on the door and turned around, eyeing Megan curiously. Megan couldn't help but tease her a little bit more because of how shy and clumsy Alex had become when she wrote her number on Megan's hand. It was a move straight out of a nineties teen movie. She quickly tucked her phone behind her back and gave Alex a quizzical look. *What are you looking at me for?*

Alex fished her phone out of her bag and turned her back to Megan, playing along as she answered, "Hello?"

"Hey, this is Megan," she said. "Do you remember me from, like, two minutes ago?"

"Umm, you're the pretty redhead, right?"

"No, I'm the *gorgeous* redhead," Megan answered with a grin. She felt another shiver of pleasure run through her and settle in her belly, and she was having entirely too much fun teasing Alex. "Anyway, I thought since there's a small chance that this might be our last day on earth, I better call you while I still can."

"How awkward would it have been if I gave you a fake number?" Alex asked, and Megan laughed.

"That would have been a really good burn," she said, walking up to Alex and joining her at the door. She ended the call and said, "That little stunt was eating up my data, and I'm a poor medical student. I couldn't afford a longer conversation."

"That's exactly what every girl wants to hear," Alex said.

"Well, the poverty thing is temporary," Megan said sarcastically. "But this gorgeous face is forever."

"Oh, and you're so modest."

"Whatever, you know you're a knock-out, too," Megan said. "In fact, I don't think we could ever be together because it would be unfair to the rest of the world, but we could probably go on a little adventure together if you're up for it."

"What do you have in mind?" Alex asked.

"Well, I might have contracted this disease, and they tell me it's contagious," Megan said. "I have to go to the pharmacy and fill an antibiotic prescription. Want to come with me?"

"Oh, yeah," Alex said. "I might have that same problem, now that you mention it."

"Perfect," Megan said, pushing the lab door open and stepping aside. "After you."

They headed back to the elevators and Megan pushed the button for the second floor, where the signs on the wall told her the pharmacy was located. She was biting her lip and considered Alex's most likely reaction if she shoved her up against the elevator wall and kissed her right then and there. But then elderly man stepped onto the elevator as the doors slid shut, breaking up Megan's fantasy.

That was okay—it was probably time to pump the breaks anyway. Megan was interested in Alex, and she would definitely be up for some casual hospital hooking up, but she should make sure that was what Alex wanted, too, before pouncing on her in the elevator.

Megan didn't have room in her life—or her heart—for anything more than a hook up, and even those could be tricky to navigate around a medical school schedule and a nosy roommate. She hadn't been with anyone besides a few one-night stands and a superficial summer fling since her one and only long-term relationship ended a year and a half ago.

"Could one of you ladies select floor one for me?" the man asked, and Alex reached forward and hit the button for him. She glanced at Megan with a hint of desire, like she might have enjoyed being pushed up against the elevator wall if they had been alone, and the tingling sensation in Megan's belly intensified. She decided to use the rest of their little impromptu adventure to find out exactly what Alex wanted, and make her own expectations clear.

They got out on the second floor and Megan read the directory again to find out where the pharmacy was, then hooked her arm around Alex's elbow to lead her toward it. Alex blushed, but she didn't move away. They made their way down a long hallway with empty gurneys lining the walls, just waiting for patients. Alex asked Megan questions about medical school—all the usual stuff that people wanted to know as soon as Megan told them she was going to be a doctor.

What did you study in undergrad? How hard is the curriculum, really? What do you want to specialize in?

Megan answered them all, mostly just rattling off the memorized answers she had been giving to her friends and relatives for years now. Then Alex threw her a curveball as she said, "This is the strangest first date I've ever been on."

"Date?" Megan asked, and she watched Alex's expression cloud self-consciously.

"Or adventure, as you called it," she added quickly. "Strangest adventure."

Megan gave her a quick laugh and decided to divert the conversation back to the playful, teasing, and not at all date-worthy tone they'd been enjoying. She didn't want to give Alex the wrong idea. She gestured to the hallway and said in a purposefully lascivious tone, "Do you want to make it the strangest hook-up you've ever had? On medical TV shows there's a call room in every hall."

"Jeez," Alex said, acting offended and rolling her eyes. "If you're not going to buy me dinner first then the least you could do is take me to the pharmacy to pick up my prescription before you put the moves on."

"What kind of girl do you think I am?" Megan asked, putting her hand to her chest in offense.

"The kind that wants to seduce me in a call room," Alex said with a smirk. Then she slipped her hand into Megan's and added, "I'm not saying I hate the idea, but we really do need to get those antibiotics or it'll be the last thing we do."

THE PHARMACY TURNED out to be even more crowded than the lab, and they ended up waiting for their prescriptions for more than twenty minutes, unable to even find two chairs together so they could sit down. They used that time to continue, in whispered tones, their conversation from the hallway. Megan could feel the blood rising in her cheeks as they continued to talk about their desire for each other in innuendos, and while she'd mentioned the call room as a joke, her whole body was eager to make good on her words. She wanted nothing more than to put her hands on Alex's hips, pull her close, and taste her lips, but their audience of sick people waiting for their prescriptions would not have appreciated a show like that, and she could only keep teasing Alex.

When they finally had their prescriptions in hand, they stood outside of the pharmacy and Megan, biting her lip and itching to get closer to Alex, asked, "What do you want to do now?"

Alex checked the time on her phone and said, "I have forty-five minutes before class starts, and it takes fifteen to get there from here. I don't have time for much."

Megan didn't want to let her go yet—not with all of that pent-up desire still simmering between them. So she said, "There's a cafeteria around here somewhere. Want to get a cup of coffee or a snack before class?"

"Sure," Alex said. "We should take our first dose of antibiotics anyway."

So they headed back down the hall in search of the cafeteria, but they didn't make it very far in that direction.

They were walking past a nurse's station, Megan thinking about taking Alex's hand again as it swung between them, when a door opened in the hall and they both had to leap out of the way to avoid being hit. Alex bumped into Megan and her pulse quickened.

"That's not very safe for a hospital," Alex murmured as a guy with wrinkled scrubs and a bad case of bedhead rushed out of the room. He was looking down at his pager and he spared a disinterested glance at Alex, then hurried down the hall.

"Medical resident," Megan guessed. "He must have gotten a code."

She nearly kept walking, but then a wicked idea grabbed hold of her. She caught the door before it could swing shut and glanced inside. There were three cots—two in bunkbed formation and one stand-alone bed—and a small end table with an alarm clock on it, but otherwise the room was empty. Arching her eyebrow at Alex, Megan took her by the hand and pulled her inside. "Come on. Quick, before someone sees us."

Alex turned her head to make sure the coast was clear, but the only other person in the hallway was a girl returning to the nurse's station who was only interested in answering the phone ringing on her desk. She didn't even notice Megan and Alex slip into the call room.

"We're going to get in trouble," Alex said as the door shut quietly behind them. "We shouldn't be in here."

"That's what makes it fun," Megan answered. She was still holding Alex's hand, rubbing her thumb over her soft skin. Alex looked flushed and nervous and excited all at the same time. It was the same way Megan felt, and she couldn't remember the last time a girl had this intense of an effect on her.

"Does this door even lock?" Alex asked nervously, reaching behind her to feel for the knob. Instead of responding, Megan leaned in and gently kissed her.

Her lips tasted as sweet as they looked, plump and tender with a faint hint of something fruity from her lip balm. The lilac smell of her hair wafted over to Megan and she wanted to melt into her. Alex forgot about the non-existent door lock and gave her attention to Megan.

She put her hand on the side of Megan's cheek, her

finger tracing the line of her jaw. Such a simple touch sent shivers all through her, and there was just something about Alex that made Megan want to go feral and tear her clothes off. But Alex was holding her back, making her go slowly, and that felt pretty good, too.

She stepped closer, putting her hands on Alex's waist as she kissed her again, slowly, sensually. She wanted to taste every inch of her and commit every second of this bliss to memory because she had no idea when she'd have time for another moment like this.

Alex put her arms around Megan's shoulders and allowed her body to come closer, the curves of her breasts grazing Megan's chest and her hips inching teasingly close to Megan's own. She exhaled, her breath hot against Megan's skin, and she was pretty sure that fruity smell from her lips was raspberries. A small moan escaped Megan's mouth and then Alex was leaning back into her, parting her lips and sliding her tongue tentatively into her mouth.

Megan felt electricity coursing through her body, concentrating between her thighs, and she squeezed Alex's hips a little tighter as she brought their tongues to touch. She took another step forward, bringing their bodies together and Alex's back to the door, and she could hear Alex's breathing grow heavier. She was enjoying this, and it was exactly what Megan needed after the last couple of difficult days. All of her concerns about class rank and med school nemeses and meningitis patients floated away, and she allowed herself to concentrate fully on the sensations of touching and kissing Alex.

There was no more need for sarcasm, or innuendos, or the pretense of a silly hospital adventure. All that was left between them was desire, and Megan pressed her lips a little more urgently against Alex's mouth.

She slid one hand beneath the hem of Alex's shirt, and her fingertips found the underwire of her bra before Alex pushed her hand away and then spun her around, turning Megan's back to the door as Megan let out a surprised, pleased little groan. She couldn't remember the last time she wanted someone this badly.

Alex slid her hands down Megan's sides, sending another wave of shivers down into Megan's core, and then her supple lips found the curve of Megan's jaw. She kissed the corner of her mouth, and then her chin, and then she left a trail of kisses all the way along Megan's jaw and down her neck to her collar bone. Megan felt her whole body igniting with desire, wondering just how far they could go in a room like this.

Alex was right, though—that door *didn't* lock, and they *shouldn't* be in there.

But Megan didn't want to be anywhere else. As soon as Alex stood upright again, smirking seductively at Megan with those steely eyes, she wrapped her arms around Alex's waist and began walking her toward one of the beds. They kissed passionately as she slowly guided Alex backward, and as soon as Alex's calves hit the mattress, her eyes popped open with alarm.

"Wait," she said.

"It's okay," Megan said reassuringly. "No one's going to walk in on us."

"You don't know that," Alex shot back, and Megan had to smile.

"You're right," she said. "But it's worth the risk, isn't it?"

She leaned back in and kissed Alex again, gently, on the lips, but when she tried to lower her onto the bed, Alex pushed her back and stepped away from the bed, saying irritably, "It's almost ten—I'm going to be late for class."

"Skip it," Megan said, or rather begged, but Alex was already heading for the door.

"I can't," she said. "I'm sorry."

And then she was gone, the door slowly shutting behind her while Megan was left alone in the call room, wondering what the hell had gone wrong.

ELEVEN

Alex power-walked out of the hospital as fast as her legs would take her. A few dozen thoughts were buzzing through her head and she desperately wanted to shut them all out.

She had felt nervous about flirting with Megan, and even a little bit guilty. It wasn't something that she'd been interested in since her dad died, and for the past year it seemed almost inappropriate to think about girls when the rest of her world had come crashing down around her. Alex thought that giving in to the temptation of Megan might feel as if she was announcing that the mourning period was over and it was time to forget about her father. She wasn't ready to move on yet, and she wasn't ready to find out what it felt like to be intimate with someone again after so long.

There was fear there, too.

Her anti-depressants had stolen her libido last year, along with most of the rest of her emotions, and that had been fine by Alex. Who wanted to think about sex in the middle of a grieving period? She always assumed her sexuality would be there when she wanted it back, but a scared little voice in the back of her mind didn't want to find out otherwise. What if she'd gone further with Megan, let her touch her, and nothing happened? What if her body was just as numb as her mind?

Five minutes in a call room with a gorgeous woman was all Alex needed to feel scared, guilty and embarrassed, and after the way she flew out of the room, she wanted to create as much distance as possible between herself and Megan.

Alex spent most of the class that day trying not to think about it—about her fear, or about the abrupt way she'd left Megan in that call room. She took meticulous notes on even the most common sense things that Mr. Chase was teaching them just to occupy her hands. The busier she was, the less opportunity her embarrassment and guilt would have to burn in her cheeks and the less she would wonder what Megan must be thinking of her hasty retreat.

By the time Mr. Chase ended class a little after noon, Alex had done her best to repress the incident. If she could forget it happened, then she wouldn't need to deal with it any further. Maybe Megan would do her a favor and forget about it, too.

Alex went home, stopping at a burger joint on the way because her mother had a weakness for the fries there. On a better day, Alex would have cooked something fresh for lunch—maybe a couple of paninis or a salad topped with chicken breast for protein. She wasn't the best cook in the world, but she'd learned a thing or two from her parents over the years and it was the least she could do to keep her mother and herself on a balanced diet.

Today, though, she was exhausted by noon and burgers would have to do.

"Ooh, is that Epic Burger?" her mother asked as soon as she came in the door. She perked up as Alex came into the living room and plopped the greasy bag down on the coffee table. "What's the occasion?"

Heartbreak and humiliation, Alex wanted to say, but she didn't dare admit that to her mother, so instead she just said, "I happened to drive past it and the line wasn't too long."

She went into the kitchen and grabbed a couple plates, coming back and passing one to her mother so they could divvy up the fries. The Home Shopping Network droned in the background as usual, just loud enough to be distracting as Alex noticed that the product of the hour was a set of LED lights for kitchen cabinets.

"Only nineteen ninety-five," the host was saying with a permanent smile stretched across his lips. "You could illuminate your whole kitchen for under a hundred bucks!"

Alex wondered if her mother had purchased them already. She didn't buy everything that came across the screen, but stuff like that was easy to justify with a thought like, *Next week I'll finally get off the couch, and installing a set of under-cabinet LED lights will give me just the motivation I need.*

In reality, the box would sit unopened in the garage along with all the other stuff she bought. Alex stopped going out there after a while because it was beginning to look like an episode of Hoarders, and she didn't like seeing her father's old hang-out spot like that. Sometimes she wondered if her mother was doing it on purpose, filling up the physical space he used to inhabit with junk to fill the void his absence had left behind.

"They offer you stock in the company yet?" Alex asked as she dug her burger out of the bottom of the bag. "You might as well invest, you're paying that host's salary anyway."

"Don't sass me," her mother said, rolling her eyes. She sat back with her burger and fries on a plate in her lap. Alex noted with slight surprise that she'd changed into a fresh pair of sweatpants, and her hair was damp from the shower. It wasn't much, but it was something, and she didn't want to give her mom a hard time.

Dana McHenry's life had come to a screeching halt the day her husband of twenty-five years passed away, and if she needed to sit on the couch and buy stupid gadgets from the television in order to deal with it, Alex wasn't going to stop her. They each had their own coping mechanisms, and she knew her mother would snap out of it when she was ready.

"I don't want to alarm you folks," the host was saying, "but we've got less than a hundred units left and these *will* sell out. If you want these fantastic under-cabinet LED lights, you better jump on it."

Alex's mother reached for her laptop with one hand while she shoved a fry in her mouth with the other. Alex let out an inaudible sigh and said, "I have homework so I'm going to eat in my room."

"Okay, baby," her mother said, opening her laptop as Alex took her plate down the hall. Just because she thought her mother needed to work through her father's death in her own way didn't mean that Alex wanted a front row seat to watch the grieving process. She'd seen enough of that already in the mirror.

TWELVE

Alex was sitting at her desk, her eyes beginning to glaze over from staring too long at her *Paramedic Care: Principles and Practice* textbook, when her phone began to ring, providing a welcome distraction.

She reached over her empty plate and picked it up, and was surprised to see that it was Megan's number. Alex hesitated for just a second, wondering how this call would go after their tumultuous morning, and then she answered.

"This *must* be a pocket dial," she said, trying to sound casual as her cheeks grew warm. She was rewarded with Megan's sweet laugh.

"Is that the same thing as a booty call?" Megan asked. "I'm not up on all the slang that kids these days use."

"I'm not that much younger than you," Alex objected. She was relieved that Megan was allowing her to skip all the awkwardness of their last encounter and instead pick right back up with the teasing tone that had quickly become habitual between them.

"How old are you, anyway?" Megan asked, and then without waiting for Alex's answer she said, "I'm going to guess eighteen."

"Fifteen," Alex answered, grinning even though no one could see it. Megan had a way of putting a smile on her face.

"Am I on a recorded line?" Megan asked. "Usually the scene with Chris Hansen happens *before* people hook up, not after."

Alex laughed and said, "I'm twenty."

"Oh boy," Megan said with a heavy sigh. "That's entirely too old for me."

Now it was Alex's turn to laugh, as she asked, "You can't be much older than that. How old are you?"

"Twenty-three," Megan said with a heavy sigh. "So you see, I'm going to have to shut this down."

"And what is this?" Alex asked coyly, her teeth grazing her lower lip as she waited anxiously for Megan's response. She was feeling jittery and a little bit lovestruck, and it took her off-guard every time she talked to Megan.

"I don't know," Megan said, and then disappointingly, she steered the conversation to the one thing Alex wanted to avoid. "I was actually calling to see if I did something wrong this morning."

"Umm," Alex hedged, wondering what to say and how honest she should be. She'd been so hopeful about skipping this talk altogether, but of course Megan would want an explanation. Alex settled on, "No, you didn't do anything wrong. It was great, actually."

"So great you couldn't stand being there a minute longer?"

"It's been a long time since I've kissed someone," Alex said, putting her hand over her face to ward off the embarrassment rising in her cheeks. This would be a much easier conversation to have in person, or with her therapist, or anyone other than the beautiful girl who had witnessed her insecurity first-hand this morning. She wondered how much she should tell Megan, but she had to say something more otherwise it would sound like she was confessing to being an inexperienced bundle of nerves. She blurted, "My dad died."

"Oh," Megan said, as surprised as Alex that's she'd said that. "I'm sorry."

"Not recently," Alex added. She had no idea why she was telling this to Megan, but she'd started it now so she had to finish the story. "It was a little over a year ago. Heart attack."

"Oh," Megan said again, and then, "I'm sorry for your loss."

Alex hated that phrase. It wasn't Megan's fault, nor any of the dozens of other people who said it to Alex and her mother in the past year, but as far as condolences went, it never did much for her. She didn't *lose* her father. He hadn't slipped between the couch cushions or wandered off at the grocery store or been left behind on the bus. But there was no better phrase available, and *I'm sorry for your loss* was just one of those things that Alex had to get used to hearing.

"Thanks," she said. "Anyway, I haven't really been with anyone since, or wanted to. I guess I freaked out a little bit."

"That's understandable," Megan said.

She paused for a long time, and then Alex quietly asked, "So what do we do now?"

"Well, I don't want to bother you if you'd rather not be bothered," Megan hedged, and Alex was quick to cut her off.

"No," she said. "Bother me, please."

This was another response she hadn't been expecting from herself. Spending the whole morning pushing away thoughts of the call room had the effect of denying Alex an opportunity to explore her feelings on the subject, and now that she had she found that the feelings of guilt were outweighed by the strange, spirit-lifting effect that Megan had on her.

She added, "I think I just need to take it slow."

"I don't mind going slow," Megan said, and now her voice had taken on the seductive tone she'd used to such great effect in the hospital earlier. "Slow can be fun."

"Thanks," Alex answered gratefully.

"Well, I have to run to a lecture in a few minutes," Megan said. "I just wanted to make sure you were okay and I didn't do something idiotic earlier. Do you want to get together again sometime, maybe outside of the hospital?"

"I'd like that," Alex said with a big, goofy grin on her face.

They hung up and Alex noticed that her phone's alarm had gone off while they were talking—it was the one she set every afternoon to remember her pill—and she went into the bathroom.

She shook one into her palm and looked into the bottom of the pill bottle. There was a possibility that it wouldn't matter how slow she and Megan went—if she kept taking these pills, she might never be able to feel their relationship, physically or emotionally. Alex was getting really tired of being numb, of merely subsisting rather than living, and Megan made her see what she was missing for the first time in a long while. Alex couldn't remember the last time she'd smiled with such genuine emotion.

She took the pill, then called her therapist to reschedule her weekly appointment to an earlier time slot. She decided it was time to remember what it was like to feel her emotions, and feel someone else's body against hers. It was time to start tapering off the pills.

THIRTEEN

"What are you smiling about?" Ivy asked, rolling her eyes as Megan narrowly avoided running into her—again.

This time, it wasn't the hospital lab. It was the door to the lecture hall, and Megan had been so preoccupied with her phone that she didn't even notice Ivy power-walking toward the door. Megan had promised Alex that they would take things slowly, but that didn't mean she could resist the urge to send her a few flirtatious texts.

It had begun the morning after they talked on the phone. Megan woke up and Alex was the first thing on her mind, but she had a full schedule ahead of her that day and no time to convince Alex that they should meet up, perhaps to continue what they'd started in the call room. So instead, she sent her a text (*I think I had a dream about you last night.*), blushed a little as she hit send, and then put her phone down as she went to take a shower and get ready for the day.

When she got back to her room twenty minutes later, a message was waiting for her.

What kind of dream?

Megan didn't have the benefit of reading Alex's expression to see whether there was flirtation behind that question, but just reading her words sent a shiver of warm desire through Megan and she wanted to believe that there was. She wrote back—*The best kind.*—and thus began a stream of nearly constant texts back and forth with the girl with the steely eyes.

When Ivy questioned her dopy expression, though, Megan snapped out of it for a moment, holding her phone down by her side and retorting, "Oh, I was just remembering the look on your face last week when Dr. Morrow corrected you in front of the class. Who at this stage in their education *doesn't* know that *carbaminohemoglobin* binds with carbon dioxide?"

"I know that," Ivy said, her teeth clenched as she spoke.

It was very obvious that Megan's words had gotten to her—it may have been less of a blow if Megan had literally punched Ivy in the gut just then—and for an instant, Megan felt bad. After a year of this rivalry, she wasn't even sure exactly why they were so relentlessly harsh with each other, but one thing was for sure—Ivy started it. Megan would have been perfectly happy to be friends, but what began with a snarky comment in the college bookstore on the first day of medical school quickly morphed into genuine animosity, and now she played along out of habit, and because she knew Ivy's next attack was never far away.

"I knew the answer wasn't *oxyhemoglobin*," Ivy went on, determined to make her point. "I just misspoke."

"Tell it to Dr. Morrow," Megan said, her phone vibrating in her hand.

She began to raise it to read the message, mostly on reflex because the conversation she and Alex were in the middle of was not something she intended to continue while she was standing in front of Ivy and they were holding up the line of students entering the lecture hall. But before she even had a chance to look at her phone, Ivy snatched it out of her hand.

"What the hell," Megan began to object, reaching for it, and Ivy read the screen. Her eyes went wide and then she scowled at Megan as she handed the phone back, letting go a moment too soon and forcing Megan to grab for it before it fell to the floor.

"Idiot," Ivy snarled at her, and then she went to the front of the room to take her customary seat in the front row.

Megan stepped out of the way of the line forming behind her, feeling irritated by Ivy and her constant snarky remarks. She sat down at a desk in the middle of the room and checked the message that had come through.

Tell me about the dream you had of me. Tell me how it made you feel ;)

A small smile formed on Megan's lips again, and even though Ivy couldn't see it from where she was sitting, Megan did her best to suppress it. On one hand, she was having a hell of a lot of fun talking to Alex, and needing to take things slow just made the anticipation that much greater. On the other hand, hadn't Megan *just* told herself less than twenty-four hours earlier that she didn't have time for Alex, or any girl for that matter? Ivy's invectives only served to remind her of that, and Megan couldn't help but wonder what the hell she was doing.

She bit her lower lip and put her thumbs to the screen, figuring that it wouldn't hurt to indulge Alex's curiosity while Megan was waiting for class to start, but before she had a chance to respond, Chloe slid into the seat beside hers.

"Hey, roomie," she chirped as she got out her laptop and prepared for class.

"Hi," Megan answered, putting her phone in her backpack as she did the same. It would be too strange to flirt with Alex while Chloe sat right next to her, and she couldn't get away with that during class, anyway. It was one thing to give some of her free time to Alex, but it was a whole other level of uncharacteristic behavior to ignore the lecture in favor of her.

"What did you think of the readings last night?" Chloe asked. "You were already in your room by the time I got home, so I didn't get a chance to ask."

Reviewing lectures and homework assignments was one of Chloe's daily rituals, which she and Megan usually did over coffee on mornings when neither of them had to run off to an early morning class. It was one of the best things about rooming with another medical student—Chloe kept Megan focused. In fact, she had pretty much the exact opposite effect that Alex had on Megan.

"Umm," she said. She *had* done the readings—she never missed an assignment, especially with Ivy lying in wait for the day that Megan showed weakness—but after her phone conversation with Alex, she'd been so distracted thinking about her that she didn't commit very much of what she read to memory. She had no choice but to make something up. "I'm looking forward to hearing Dr. Morrow's take on that bacterial respiratory infection article. What about you?"

Chloe started rattling off her impressions and thoughts on the article, and Megan felt guilty for not having a better answer. She wasn't prepared for this class like she wanted to be, and if she wanted to keep her class rank, that couldn't happen again. Dr. Morrow approached the podium at the head of the room and Megan pulled out her notes on the respiratory system. They were nearly halfway done with this module already, and the semester was beginning to really fly by.

AFTER CLASS, Chloe headed across campus to do some research for the end-of-module paper that would be due around Thanksgiving, and Megan headed back to the apartment. As soon as she was alone, she dug her phone out of her backpack and returned to her conversation with Alex. As much as she had told herself to pay attention during Dr. Morrow's lecture and push Alex out of her mind, Megan had been unsuccessful.

She wasn't really sure what it was about Alex that made her so interesting. Maybe it was the effortless way that they spoke to each other—usually when Megan met someone knew, there was a period of awkwardness while they became accustomed to each other, but with Alex, it was instantaneous. Or maybe it was the silent strength that Megan could feel whenever she was around Alex. There was something about her that said she'd been hurt, but that she was strong enough to overcome anything the world threw at her. Megan was drawn to that, because at least in the romance department, she felt very much the opposite.

Her first and only long-term relationship, with a girl named Ruby who she grew up with, fell in love with, went to college with, had ended in a spectacular explosion of pain and hurt feelings, and Megan had been largely to blame for it. Now she was afraid to get close to someone new lest she replay that whole story again and hurt someone else the way she hurt Ruby. Megan knew she should keep her distance from Alex, for both of their sakes, but it was hard to do when she couldn't stop thinking about her.

She responded to Alex's last text, asking for details of her dream.

Well, it started in a hospital call room...

FOURTEEN

The next time Alex and Megan met was about a week and a half after their hospital adventure, and the mid-October air had become colder as Alex headed to Northwestern's library. She was very busy, between classes and labs and research assignments, and Alex had her own schedule to keep to, so in the end it was easiest for Alex to meet Megan after one of her daily study sessions. The university library was far bigger and more comprehensive than the small room full of reference books and computer terminals that was the library at Evanston Community College, and Alex counted herself lucky to find Megan at all in the maze of shelves and study carrels.

"There you are," Megan said as she approached, shutting her laptop and standing to greet her. "Find it okay?"

"Eventually," Alex said with a laugh. Megan's small desk was piled with books and Alex nodded to them, asking, "What are you studying?"

"The nervous system," Megan said. "It's never too early to start preparing for exams, and I'm also doing a literature review for my research project. I decided to dig a little further into the meningitis case we saw and I've been talking to one of the interns who worked in the ER the day that Paul Goulding was there."

"That case really intrigued you," Alex observed.

"It's just kind of crazy that there could be a bacterium out there that's strong enough to kill someone in such a short time, and yet no one even recognized it until the autopsy," Megan said. Then she shook her head and said, "Anyway, we were going to get coffee. You ready?"

"Yep," Alex said with a smile. "We never did make it to the hospital cafeteria, so I think you owe me one."

"I owe *you*?" Megan asked, raising a skeptical eyebrow. "How do you figure?"

"You're the one that got amorous in the call room," Alex pointed out.

"I seem to remember you enjoying that moment, too," Megan said, and Alex blushed, suddenly aware of the other people in the study carrels around them.

"Shh," she said, but they all just kept their heads down and she added with a smirk, "Fine, I'll buy."

"I was just teasing," Megan said as she scooped up her laptop and some loose papers and started putting them in her backpack. "I'd love to buy you a cup of coffee, as long as you don't drink that sugary unicorn crap that costs seven dollars a cup."

"Oh, I forgot," Alex said, tapping her fingernail on

the cover of Megan's expensive laptop as she slid it into her bag. "You're broke."

"Completely," Megan said. "I had to smash my piggy bank to take you out today, so you better be happy with a small black coffee."

"I'll do my best to be a cheap date," Alex said, shooting her a smile. It was always so easy to banter with Megan, and so much fun to push her buttons.

She watched Megan pick up the remaining books on her desk and carry them over to a book cart at the end of an aisle, and then Megan waved Alex over, saying, "Hey, come here. I want to show you something."

"What?" Alex asked, following her into the stacks.

Megan reached for her hand, sending excitement rushing into Alex's cheeks. They'd spent a whole week sending flirtatious text messages back and forth to each other, and it was nice to feel Megan's hand in hers after all that built-up tension.

They made it about halfway down the row before Megan whispered her reply. "This."

And then she pulled Alex into a slow, smoldering kiss. Alex felt her cheeks growing even warmer, her whole body tingling from the softness of Megan's lips. She'd missed that feeling, and she was apprehensive about it, too. What if Megan didn't want to go slow, or wasn't content with the flirtatious text messages they'd been exchanging? Alex's heart leaped into her throat every time she saw Megan's name flash across her phone screen, but she didn't know how her body would react to her in person. She'd made a plan with her therapist to taper off her anti-depressants—she was ready to re-enter the world of the living as long as Megan helped her ease into it. But it would take a while to get all the medication out of her system, and in the back of her mind there was the lingering fear that she had sacrificed her sexual drive for a little bit of numbness.

It had been so long since anything really felt good, and Megan was so beautiful, so seductive, it scared Alex.

She pulled away from the kiss, intent on coming clean to Megan about the reason why she'd asked to take things slow, but before she got the chance, she heard someone clear their throat at the end of the aisle. Alex took a step away from Megan and they both turned to look at the source of the interruption—a petite girl with a comically large pile of medical textbooks in her arms who had paused at the end of the row to glower at them.

"Crap," Megan muttered as she caught sight of her, and they exchanged scowls before the girl went on her way.

"You know her?" Alex asked when she was gone.

"She's my med school nemesis, Ivy," Megan said. Then, shaking it off, she reached for Alex's hand again. "Should we go get that coffee?"

"Yeah," Alex answered, grateful for this little interruption because she hadn't quite gotten up the courage to tell this gorgeous, bewitching girl her darkest secrets. She added, "We better go before she reports us to a librarian."

FIFTEEN

The coffee shop was busy when they arrived. Despite teasing Alex about drinking cheap black coffee, Megan ordered a mocha with extra whipped cream and chocolate drizzle—her favorite—and Alex ended up going for the plain brewed coffee after all.

"You know you can order whatever you want," Megan said as she pulled out her bank card. "I was teasing about the piggy bank."

"I know," Alex said. "But I actually like regular coffee, and apparently you're the hypocrite with a penchant for sugary unicorn drinks."

"What can I say? I like my coffee like my women—sweet and covered in whipped cream," Megan answered with a grin.

They found a couple of comfortable chairs near the back of the café and sat down. The rest of the coffee shop patrons moved around them, coming and going while Megan and Alex stayed put. They talked for a long time, finishing conversations started in text and beginning ne. ones, and most of their topics came back around to flirtation in some way or another. Megan was more comfortable that way—she didn't have time to date, or the desire to, and if all they were doing was flirting, it would be easier for her to enjoy this moment instead of questioning it.

"So what kind of meningitis research are you doing?" Alex asked as she sipped her coffee and Megan licked the whipped cream off of hers. That was another good reason to order a sugary drink, because she took a perverse amount of pleasure in watching the way Alex's eyes zeroed in on her tongue, and the way she squirmed slightly—almost imperceptibly—at the sight.

Megan smiled, washed down her mouthful of whipped cream with a sip of her drink, and said, "I'm mostly interested in the course of the disease, particularly the way that it spreads from one person to another. Did you know that there only has to be one more case of the same strain in order for the Centers for Disease Control to officially consider it an outbreak?"

"No," Alex said. "That seems so minor."

"Not for something as lethal as bacterial meningitis," Megan said. "There are a lot of different bacteria that cause it and not much protection against it. If one person gets sick, everyone in the community is at risk."

"That's pretty scary," Alex said.

"Just keep taking your antibiotics and you'll be fine," Megan said, enjoying the way this doctorly advice sounded coming out of her mouth.

:en researching the disease all week and knew

ɔf contracting it were slim, but she could

ɔw worrisome it might be to someone without

that ⌐ɪ ialized knowledge. She thought it might be a good idea to change the subject—to avoid scaring Alex and also because bacterial meningitis didn't make the best bedroom talk—but Alex spared her the trouble of thinking of something new to talk about.

"I can see how passionate you are about all of this," she said. "What made you want to become a doctor?"

"My mom's an acute care nurse," Megan said. "She used to bring me to the hospital on Take Your Daughter to Work Day when I was a kid and I was always fascinated with all the people who were there just because they wanted to help others get better. Granted, bodily functions aren't really my thing, so I when I got older I decided that being a doctor meant less chance of getting puked on than being a nurse like my mom."

Alex laughed, and then Megan went on.

"That's not the only reason I chose medical school, but I'd be lying if I said it didn't weigh into my decision," she said. "You, on the other hand, are probably going to be elbow-deep in bodily functions as a paramedic."

"God willing," Alex said, laughing again and putting her hands together as if in prayer.

"You're a sick individual," Megan said, grinning at her.

Alex asked, "What do you have to do to become a doctor, anyway?"

Megan let out a sigh and then laughed. "A lot."

"Tell me," Alex said, her lips curling into a very subtle smile.

"Well, you start with an undergraduate degree, and once you pass the MCAT exam, you get to choose a medical school," Megan said. "I went to Northwestern for both. In medical school, you take two years of lecture-style classes on campus—I'm in my second year of that—and then you do rotations at a hospital for another two years before you earn your degree. After that, it's a three to five-year residency during which you pick your specialty, and then *finally*—if you pass your board exams —you're licensed to practice medicine."

"Wow, you're going to be an old woman before all that's through," Alex said teasingly. "So what are you going to specialize in?"

"I'm not sure yet," Megan said. "I guess it will depend on how the rotations go, but my interests are definitely piqued when it comes to pathology. I might be a future Dr. Markovich, a Medical Examiner. What about you? Why EMT school?"

"Well, it's kind of a long story," Alex said.

"My schedule's wide open until four o'clock," Megan offered.

"Alright," Alex said, but she didn't start right away. She shook her mostly-empty coffee cup and said, "I don't have enough caffeine in my system for this story. You want another?"

"Nah," Megan said, curious at Alex's sudden agitation. She wondered if she had made a mistake in asking that, and whether it would evoke the same flight response as the call room had. Alex didn't run, though. She went to the front of the café and refilled her cup from the carafes near the counter, then came back and sat down with a deep breath.

"Well," she said, taking a sip. "I guess I have to start at the beginning, two years ago. It was my first year of college and I was studying middle-grade art education at the University of Illinois."

She paused for a long time, and Megan guessed what was waiting in the silence. When she was sure that Alex wasn't going to continue of her own accord, Megan asked quietly, "And then your dad died?"

"Yeah," Alex said. Her voice was very matter-of-fact, like she was telling someone else's story. "It happened right before the start of my sophomore year. I took a semester off because I couldn't bear to go on with my life like nothing happened, and I didn't go back to school in the spring either because my mom still needed me. I was going to therapy and... well, I was taking anti-depressants. They made me numb so I could keep functioning, but my mother was the one who really fell apart. I left school to take care of her and do the things that she and my dad used to do back when we were whole people—paying bills, buying groceries, that kind of stuff."

"She's lucky to have you," Megan said, not entirely sure what to say that would be of comfort. She wondered if she should have just kept talking about meningitis instead of forcing this traumatic story out of Alex, but she hadn't thought much of the question at the time. Now, the connection between Alex's decision to become an

EMT and her father's death was obvious and Megan wondered why she didn't see it before—the way she'd looked away when the ambulance pulled into the loading bay of the Medical Examiner's Office should have been a big, flashing sign.

"I'm lucky to have her, too," Alex went on. "She's the one that encouraged me to get my life back on track, even if she's not ready to do the same yet. She wanted me to go back to the university but I couldn't imagine moving back into the dorms. My mom spends most of her days compulsively buying junk from the Home Shopping Network as her way of coping and if I left her alone, she'd end up building an As Seen On TV tomb around herself."

Megan reached over and took Alex's hand, then asked, "So why EMT school? I think that would be the last profession I'd want if I went through what you did."

Alex told her about the paramedics that responded for her father, and what a big impact they had on her. She said they were fast and skilled, and also empathetic and comforting to her, and that the best thing she could do with her life was to try and give back that kind of support to other people who were going through similar tragedies.

"They were just doing their job, trying to help my dad," she said, "but they made it a little bit easier for me to get through the worst day of my life, and I'll never forget that."

"That's really noble," Megan said, squeezing Alex's hand.

SIXTEEN

Suddenly, Alex got a little agitated, taking her hand back and fidgeting in her chair. "While we're on dark subjects, I think I should tell you something that I've been kind of avoiding. I didn't want to mention it but I feel like I probably should."

"Okay," Megan said, not sure what to expect.

Alex took a deep breath, then said, "This feels so awkward to say, but I've been having so much fun texting you this past week and I don't want you to think I'm leading you on."

"What's wrong?"

"I told you the anti-depressants I'm on make me numb," Alex said.

"Yeah," Megan nodded.

"Everywhere," Alex said, feeling like she ought to just crawl underneath the nearest table and disappear. How mortifying it was to admit such a thing to this beautiful girl who she'd been sending increasingly flirtatious texts to for days and days. She peeked up at Megan to see how she was taking it, and maybe it was the medical training kicking in, but Megan had a pretty good poker face on. Alex soldiered on, saying, "I just wanted you to know that I'm having a lot of fun getting to know you, but our texts have been so flirtatious that I just didn't want you to get the wrong idea."

"Okay," Megan said. "So you're saying that you don't want to fool around with me because you wouldn't feel anything if we did."

"This is officially more embarrassing than your moment in the autopsy suite," Alex said. Why on earth had she felt the need to admit all of this? She wished they could just go back to talking about nonsense, like Megan's medical school nemesis or her penchant for sugary unicorn drinks.

"It's not a big deal," Megan tried to reassure her. "I mean, we should probably put the brakes on, anyway."

Alex's heart fell into her gut. This was exactly the reaction she'd been afraid of. She felt like it was important to be honest with Megan, but she knew there was a possibility that finding out just how messed up Alex was would push her away. And now she was taking a big metaphorical step back away from Alex.

"We should?"

"Medical school is *really* demanding," Megan said. "I have to give it pretty much every single one of my waking hours, and it sounds like you have a pretty full plate yourself, between school and everything you do for your mother."

"I could make room for you," Alex offered quietly. She wished she could just go backward in time by about ten minutes and decide not to tell Megan about her sexual dysfunction. It had been too much, too soon, and it was ruining every nice moment they'd had in the past week. Alex had so few nice moments lately, she couldn't afford to lose any of them.

"I guess I should tell you," Megan said, "since we're doing the whole full-disclosure thing, I don't really date. I don't do relationships."

"Okay," Alex said, and then she wasn't sure what else there was left for them to discuss. She'd just thrown a cherry bomb into the fragile beginnings of their relationship, and now it felt like there was nothing left except shards of porcelain. She shrugged and said, "I should probably go. I have to study, and I'm sure you do, too."

"Oh, okay," Megan answered with a strained smile.

"Thanks for the coffee," Alex said.

"You're welcome," Megan said, trying to stand up before Alex was gone, but by the time she had shuffled her drink onto a little side table and stood, Alex was already walking away.

Megan drained the last of her coffee and then headed back to campus, walking at a leisurely pace because she still had almost an hour before her evening lab was scheduled to begin. There were a lot of conflicting emotions running through her head about Alex, and she really was at a loss to determine exactly how she felt about her.

For a moment, she thought it might be wise to explain her history with Ruby. Alex had opened up to her about her father's death and her struggle to overcome the grief that accompanied it, and Megan was sure that Alex would have listened just as attentively to Megan's own struggles. But what good would it do to explain to her why they couldn't be together? Megan just needed her to understand that she wasn't capable of being in a relationship—that was all. She didn't need to bring all of the skeletons out of her closet and put them on parade for Alex's sake.

Megan felt frustrated by the time she got back to the academic building where her lab would be held. Alex had just told her that she was incapable of having a casual relationship, of hooking up, and Megan was incapable of the exact opposite, a committed relationship. Where did that leave them?

Ever since she ended things with her first serious girlfriend, Ruby, she was all hook-ups, all the time. The closest she'd gotten to having a girlfriend was during the previous summer, when she'd spent most of her break in bed with a cute girl who lived two thousand miles away and was only in Chicago for the summer. They both knew it was nothing more than a summer fling, though.

She wasn't the slightest bit interested in replaying the disaster of a breakup that she'd experienced when her relationship with Ruby had ended. She'd handled it so badly, abruptly pushing Ruby out of her life because she felt like it would be easier if it was sudden, and all she'd managed to do was hurt Ruby ten times more and damage a lifelong friendship.

Megan didn't want that coffee shop date to be the last

she saw of Alex, but maybe it would be better if it was. She was telling the truth when she said she didn't have time for anything except school.

ALEX'S next class was difficult, piling on to the confusion that she felt about how her coffee date with Megan ended.

Mr. Chase spent over an hour giving a lecture on cardiac emergencies, covering symptoms that Alex knew all too well. He discussed the paramedic's role in treatment, and the majority of the things he listed would have been inapplicable for her father.

Calm the patient. Administer nitroglycerin and/or aspirin. Not for someone who was unresponsive by the time the ambulance arrived.

CPR for those in cardiac arrest with no breathing or pulse. That was more like it.

Alex was only too happy to bolt out of the building when class was finished, speed walking to her car as fast as her legs could carry her. Somewhere behind her, Sarah was calling after her—she probably wanted to schedule a study session for their upcoming test—but Alex couldn't take being on campus a minute longer.

Her chest was feeling tight and her pulse was racing, mimicking the symptoms that Mr. Chase had just described in such vivid detail, except hers were a byproduct of panic, not cardiac arrest. That wasn't something Alex was used to, and she could feel the effects of tapering off her medication already. Her therapist had said it would take a few weeks, and that she shouldn't expect it to be easy, but Alex hadn't been prepared for a day like this. She headed straight for her car and made a mental note to call Sarah later to find out what she wanted.

She reached for the radio and turned on the angriest music she could find, playing it just loud enough that the vibrations from her stereo mixed with the anxiety in her body and made it impossible to tell the two apart. It seemed counterintuitive to lean into the feeling, but after a few minutes of driving down the road with the screeching vocals and heavy vibrations of a metal band, Alex felt calmer. She was having to relearn all of the coping skills that had been rendered irrelevant thanks to the little blue pills that blotted out her emotions, and now they were flooding back in the most unpleasant ways.

By the time Alex got home, her breathing had returned to normal and the anxiety in her chest was nearly gone. She went inside and sighed as she leaned against the doorway to the living room.

Her mother was curled up beneath a lap blanket to ward off the cooler weather, and a pizza box lay open on the coffee table in front of her, a few slices missing. Otherwise, this tableau was exactly the same as Alex always expected to find it, and the product of the hour was a hundred-piece survival kit, complete with a bucket full of freeze-dried and powdered entrees that the host was trying in vain to make appetizing.

"This chicken noodle casserole cooks instantly with

just a half-cup of hot water," she was saying, lifting her spoon and not quite getting up the nerve to taste it on the air.

"Hey, ma," Alex said. "Order anything good today?"

"They had a really nice Tupperware set a few hours ago," she said. "Twenty-four pieces, dishwasher safe, BPA-free."

"Cool," Alex said. They had at least three other sets stuffed into cabinets in the kitchen, but she didn't have the energy to hassle her mother about her coping mechanisms today. She came into the living room and asked, "Mind if I join you?"

"Of course, sweetie," her mom said, gathering up her blanket and clearing a cushion for Alex. "There's pizza if you want it. It's just delivery, nothing fancy."

"Thanks," Alex said, grabbing a lukewarm slice out of the box.

She ate in silence for a minute or two, watching the Home Shopping Network host heat water in an electric kettle and then demonstrate how a survivalist would reconstitute a packet of peach cobbler. At least that one looked like something you might logically add hot water to.

"So, umm, we talked about cardiac emergencies today in class," Alex said after she'd finished her first slice of pizza and reached for another one. "It was kind of rough."

"I tried to warn you," her mother said, and Alex was surprised to find that her tone was more concerned than judgmental. "I still think you should re-enroll in your art education program. You love teaching."

"I used to love it," Alex said. "But things happen and plans change. I think I'm on the right course now, even if it's hard sometimes."

Her mother didn't answer right away, her eyes going back to the television screen where everything was safe and the world made sense as long as she just kept waiting for deals. With a deep breath, Alex reached for the remote and watched her mom's hand flinch.

She turned off the TV and her mom said, "Please turn that back on. I was watching it."

"In a minute, ma. I want to talk," Alex said.

It was her mother's insistence that she get back to living her life that caused Alex to enroll in the EMT program in the first place, and now even though Megan had broken off whatever it was they were doing and she'd just had a panic attack in her car, she was finally beginning to crawl out of the cocoon she'd wrapped around herself last year. She thought it was time for her mother to begin to do the same, and if she needed someone to kick her into gear too, then Alex was going to try.

"It's going to sell out," her mother said a little more insistently, irritation edging into her voice. "That means they're about to introduce a new product. Turn it back on."

"In a minute," Alex said. "I think you've been watching too much of this crap."

"It's not crap."

"The entire garage is filled with junk we're never going to use," Alex said. "Ma, you have to get off the couch. You need to go back to work and get on with your life."

Her mother snatched the remote out of Alex's hand and flipped the television back on. They were still on the survival kit, but a countdown timer had been added to the bottom of the screen just like she predicted.

"They're not holding my job anymore," she said. "I lost it months ago."

"I know," Alex said. "You could apply for a new job, find something part-time at first."

"Not today," she muttered, cradling the remote protectively in her lap.

"Okay, ma," Alex said. She was still holding a slice of uneaten pizza, but she had no appetite for it anymore. She put it back in the box and stood up. "I'm sorry."

She went down the hall to her room and closed the door gently, then collapsed on her bed, looking up at the ceiling. A single hot tear fell down the side of her face, and then another, and then she squeezed her eyes shut. This whole *living her life without anti-depressants* thing was going to be harder than she thought, especially if she couldn't get her mother on board.

SEVENTEEN

The following morning, Megan awoke to her phone ringing. She jerked out of sleep, snatching the phone off her dresser and answering without looking at the caller ID because no one ever called her so early in the morning. With all the anxiety and precautions surrounding the meningitis exposure, she was half worried that someone was calling to deliver her bad news.

"Hello?"

"Hey, Megan," an unfamiliar female voice said, and it was friendly in a way that made it pretty unlikely that this was the bad kind of early morning phone call. "It's Krys Stevens from Lakeside Hospital. Do you remember me?"

"Oh, hi Krys," Megan said, relaxing. "Yes, of course."

She'd gone back to the hospital a few days ago to steal a few more minutes of Dr. Stevens' time. They talked about the precautions that the ER had taken after their unwitting exposure to meningitis. Once again, Dr.

Stevens had been pulled away when an ambulance arrived, but Megan had given Krys her phone number in case she remembered any more details of the case for her research paper.

"I wanted to let you know we had a second case of bacterial meningitis last night," Krys said. "A fifteen-year-old who was rushed in with a high fever and vomiting after he left football practice."

"Oh no," Megan said.

"He's going to be fine," Krys added quickly. "His treatment was started in time and we're expecting him to make a full recovery."

"Oh, good," Megan said with relief. "So was it the same strain of bacteria?"

"Yep, *Neisseria*," Krys said. "His school is taking this very seriously. They want to avoid any chance of the disease spreading further, so we're going to take swabs and order antibiotics for the entire student body, as well as the staff. I figured you'd be interested to hear about it, and if you're available, we could use extra help on swab day. Are you interested?"

"Hell yeah," Megan said, putting her hand self-consciously to her mouth as she realized that was a less than professional response. She asked, "When?"

"First thing tomorrow," Krys said. "We had to get the antibiotics shipped in because we don't normally have large quantities like that on hand, but we can't put it off long. We've already distributed an information sheet to parents so they can look out for any suspicious symptoms in the meantime. So you're in?"

"Absolutely," Megan said. She grabbed a sheet of paper off her desk and jotted down the details, including the school's address, and then hung up the phone with a huge grin on her face. This would make for an excellent learning opportunity, and a very compelling research project that would certainly upstage whatever inconsequential literature review Ivy turned in.

The first thing Megan did was send an email to Dr. Morrow explaining why she would be absent from his lecture tomorrow. The second thing she did was call Alex. She knew she shouldn't do anything to draw Alex back into the romantic direction that they'd been going in, but Megan still liked her as a friend and this would be a fantastic learning experience for her, too.

"What are you doing tomorrow?" Megan asked before Alex even had a chance to say hello.

"Well, there's no class tomorrow so I guess that means it's grocery shopping day," Alex said, sounding a little wary of Megan's upbeat tone. "Why? What are *you* doing tomorrow?"

"*We* are going on a field trip," Megan said. "You can grocery shop afterward."

"Okay," Alex said warily. "Umm, about the coffee shop—"

"Do you think we could just be friends?" Megan asked. "I really like you, but it sounds like between us we have too much baggage for anything more."

"Yeah," Alex said slowly. "I guess that sounds like a good idea."

Megan filled Alex in on the details of swab day, then

she hung up to let Alex get to class. Going into the kitchen to grab a quick breakfast before heading to the library as usual, Megan ran into Chloe. She was in the middle of her own morning routine, leaning over the kitchen counter and studying her notes while she waited for the coffee to brew. When Megan walked in, she immediately looked up and smiled at her.

"Good morning, sunshine," she said. "What's on your agenda today?"

"Nothing much," she said. "Class as usual, then studying as usual. You?"

It *was* kind of nice to get back into the routine of studying. She'd underestimated the amount of time she'd spent talking to—and thinking about—Alex last week, and it was time to buckle down and think about protecting her class rank.

"Same," Chloe said. "I'm really looking forward to Dr. Morrow's lecture on proteinase-activated receptors in the respiratory system."

"Yeah," Megan said, "I've been looking forward to it all week."

Chloe went over to the coffee pot and filled a travel mug, then asked Megan if she wanted one. Megan nodded and Chloe filled hers up, too, carefully mixing in the exact proportion of cream and sugar that Megan liked. She thought briefly about not inviting Chloe to swab day tomorrow. Dr. Stevens had said they needed all the help they could get, and that she could bring her medical school friends, but there was something about letting Chloe interact with Alex that unsettled her.

It was silly, of course, because she wouldn't think twice about introducing Chloe to any of her other platonic friends. She reasoned that it was just because she couldn't immediately turn off her attraction for Alex. Deciding to be friends with her wasn't the same as flipping a switch and no longer wanting to be with her—it would just take time.

"Hey," she said casually as Chloe handed her the mug. "There was another meningitis case last night. I guess the high school is testing its entire student body just to be safe and I'm going to help with the swabs. Do you want to come?"

"When?" Chloe asked as she went over to the dining table and started to pack up her books for the day's classes.

"Tomorrow," Megan said. "First thing in the morning."

"During lecture?"

"Yeah," Megan answered.

Chloe looked at her as if she'd just suggested that they go outside and slash some tires instead of asking her to skip a lecture class. She looked a little disappointed as she said, "No, I better skip it. Have fun."

And for some irritating reason, Megan felt relieved.

EIGHTEEN

The next day, Alex woke up with more purpose than she'd felt in a long time. Megan picked her up in front of her house before the sun had risen to drive over to the high school. Megan was wearing her white coat and glowing with excitement, eager to get some practical experience, and Alex was relieved to have another chance at undoing the mess she'd created when they were in the coffee shop. She didn't want to push Megan away, and spending the day as friends, getting a little practical work experience at the same time, seemed like a good enough start toward that goal.

"Are you sure it's okay if I help?" Alex asked as they pulled into a packed parking lot. "I'm just a student."

"So am I," Megan said, shooting her a butterfly-inducing smile across the center console.

It made Alex nostalgic for their brief flirtation, but she was critically low on friends—she couldn't afford to reject Megan's suggestion that they cool things off for a while. It was probably a good idea, anyway—Megan was right about Alex's issues, but she wondered about the baggage that Megan alluded to as her own. Was a bad breakup really enough to turn Megan off dating permanently? She couldn't think about that now, though, because they were about to head into the fray.

"You're a *medical* student," Alex said. "It's different."

"Well, you're a third of the way to being an EMT," Megan pointed out. "I'm not even close to a third of the way to being a doctor. Besides, we're just going to be swabbing people all day. You're not afraid of getting puked on, are you?"

"No," Alex said, remembering their conversation from the coffee shop and shooting back, "Are you?"

"I would always prefer not to be," Megan said with a laugh, "but I'm not afraid. Come on."

They went inside and found the gymnasium, which had been temporarily converted into a treatment center. There were row upon row of tables set up in the large space, a masked volunteer sitting at each one. A couple hundred students were sitting in the bleachers, waiting for their turn to be swabbed and sent back to class.

"Wow," Alex said, taking in the scene. "It's like the beginning of an outbreak movie in here."

"They don't seem too concerned," Megan said, nodding at the students in the bleachers. She was right—most of them were laughing with their friends, or texting, or just enjoying this interruption to their class schedules.

As Alex scanned the crowd, a thin woman with dark, glossy hair pulled back into a ponytail approached them, giving Megan a grin that briefly stirred something akin to jealousy in Alex's stomach.

"Alex, this is Dr. Stevens," Megan said, making the introduction.

"Krys, please," the doctor answered, shaking Alex's hand and then gesturing around the gym. "Well, what do you think?"

"Pretty impressive," Megan said.

"Overwhelming," Alex squeaked, and they both gave her a little chuckle.

"Alex is an EMT student. I brought her along since you said you'd take extra volunteers," Megan said. "So how can we help?"

"Grab a table and start swabbing kids," Krys said.

She led them over to an open table near the bleachers and showed them how to check off each student's name on a printed list and then label the swab vials for analysis at the lab. Then she waved their first student over, demonstrated the swabbing technique, and walked away to make sure the whole operation was running smoothly.

"Well, she's efficient," Alex said with a laugh as she labeled the swab that Krys had handed her and then put the vial in a box at the end of the table.

"She has to be," Megan said. "She works in the ER."

They sent their first kid reluctantly back to his calculus class, despite protestations that he'd rather have a dozen more swabs, and then Megan waved the next one over. *Check mark. Swab. Label. Dismiss.* They repeated this process, working effectively as a team for about an hour.

Just when Alex thought that the crowd on the bleachers was beginning to dwindle, a new set of students came and filled them back up again and she realized that they were being sent to the gym in shifts. That was okay, though, because as repetitive as the work was, Megan made it fun. She chatted with the students and teased Alex about her penmanship on the vials ("You try to write on something that's half an inch wide and cylindrical," Alex retorted) and the time flew by.

It was a little after eleven when Alex couldn't ignore her need for a break any longer, leaving Megan to happily keep swabbing while Alex searched for the restroom. She was just washing her hands at the sink when a girl rushed into the room, heading into the nearest stall and slamming the door. Alex tensed, wondering if she was about to be sick, but instead she heard the faint sounds of crying—the girl was clearly trying her best to conceal her tears.

Alex went over to the stall door, feeling awkward as she knocked on it and said, "Hey, are you alright?"

"Yeah," the girl said. "Can you just, like, go away?"

"Umm, yeah I can," Alex said, but she didn't move. It seemed wrong to just leave her crying in there without any idea what was wrong. If she'd just broken up with her boyfriend or something like that, then her friends would be along shortly to comfort her. If it was anything more serious, then Alex didn't know how she felt about leaving her alone. "Do you want to talk?"

"Not really," the girl said, a sharp teenager's attitude cutting into her voice.

Alex took a step away, about to leave after all, when the stall door opened and the girl came out. This time when she spoke, Alex could hear fear and panic that were all too familiar. "You're one of the doctors, aren't you?"

"I'm an EMT student," Alex said. "Is everything okay?"

"I just *know* I have meningitis," the girl said, pacing in front of the sinks and wringing her hands with nervous energy.

"What are your symptoms?" Alex asked tentatively, not quite sure how to approach this situation. She tried to remember the list of symptoms that Megan had told her the other day.

"I don't know," the girl said irritably. "I just, like, *don't feel good*. And that boy that had it hospital sits *right* in front of me in fourth period. I know he gave it to me."

"Did you ever let him take a sip of your drink, or kiss him, or anything like that?" Alex asked.

"Eww," the girl answered in lieu of a response, continuing to pace back and forth. She was clearly in the middle of a panic attack, her mascara streaked from her crying jag and her whole body quivered as she walked. She looked exactly the way Alex felt the other day after her lesson on cardiac arrest, and she knew she had to calm the girl down.

"Well, the reason I ask is that meningitis is kind of like the kissing disease. You have to have prolonged, close contact with an infected person, or exchange bodily fluids like saliva with them, in order to catch it," Alex said, silently thanking Megan for filling her head with meningitis facts. "So the odds are pretty low that he could have given it to you just because you sit near each other. Do you have a fever, nausea, stiff neck?"

"No," the girl said.

"And did you get your swab already?"

She shook her head and said, "I didn't want them to tell me I was dying."

"I really don't think that's going to happen," Alex said. "But it's pretty important to get tested, and I'm sure it will ease your mind. Come on, I'll walk with you."

The girl rolled her eyes, as if this gesture was too juvenile for her, but she went to the sink and fixed her makeup, then followed Alex back down the hall to the gym. Megan caught Alex's eye as they entered, smiling at her from across the room before she turned back to her latest patient. That look sent a wave of desire through Alex, and she had no choice but to ignore it. She led her panicked student over to the nearest table and was surprised when the girl grabbed her hand as one of the other volunteers swabbed her throat.

As soon as it was over, she released Alex's hand as if it were the most revolting thing she'd touched all day and paused only long enough to say, "Thanks."

Then she went back to class and Alex went over to Megan's table, a big grin on her face.

"What was that all about?" Megan asked as she waved the next student over.

"I helped someone today," Alex said with a satisfied smile.

"You helped a couple hundred people today," Megan

pointed out, nodding to the nearly full box of vials on the table. Then she pointed to the rapidly emptying bleachers and said, "It looks like we'll be done pretty soon and I'm starving. You want to get something to eat?"

"I'd love that," Alex said as Megan instructed the next kid to open his mouth and say *ahh*.

THEY ENDED up at a diner down the street from the high school. As they ate, Alex told Megan about helping the girl through her panic attack and how reaffirming it had been, and Megan told Alex how many times she'd made someone gag that day.

"Fifty-seven," she said with mock pride, "but not a single actual puker."

"That might be a world record," Alex said. "We should call Guinness."

"Nah, did you see how ruthless the lady working the table next to us was? I'm sure she had way more gaggers," Megan said.

"Well, there's always the next outbreak," Alex said, laughing with Megan in a way that started in her belly and expanded until her sides ached and she felt herself losing control. She hadn't laughed that deeply or that freely in ages, and when it finally subsided, Alex sighed and looked across the table at Megan. She was incredible.

"What?" Megan asked, noting Alex's changed expression.

"I had a lot of fun with you today," she said. "More

fun than I was expecting to have swabbing a bunch of teenagers' throats."

"And that's a bad thing?" Megan asked.

Alex shrugged and said, "I don't want to just be friends with you."

"Yeah," Megan said with a sympathetic smile. "I am pretty irresistible, aren't I?"

Alex laughed and said, "Thanks for ruining the moment. I'm better now."

Megan laughed, but Alex couldn't let the moment fade away. She had to say something, so she blurted, "I'm tapering off my meds."

"You are?" Megan asked, surprised.

"Yeah," Alex said. "It's kind of a long process, but in a couple of weeks they'll be out of my system completely."

"You're not doing it for me, are you?" Megan asked, looking down at her plate and pushing her food around self-consciously.

"Kind of, yeah," Alex said. "I mean, not just for you, but because of you. You're the first person who has made me want to not be numb in a very long time."

"That's good," Megan said, smiling, but Alex could see guardedness in her eyes. When she tried to reach across the table to touch Megan's hand, she drew it away and said, "I would make a terrible girlfriend. I'm always studying and the truth of the matter is that for the next few years, medical school *has* to come first in my life."

"I don't mind coming second," Alex said, and then the scandalized look that Megan shot her made her blush instantly. She'd stumbled into yet another innuendo and

Megan never missed the opportunity to tease her about them.

"Good to know," she said. "But I just can't do it."

"Why not?"

"I don't want to hurt you," Megan said.

"Is this about your last breakup?" Alex asked, remembering what Megan had said in the coffee shop. That felt like ages ago, and on the other hand, they hadn't been able to keep up the 'just friends' charade for very long at all before they came back around to this point. It had only been a couple of weeks, and they were both still holding each other at arm's length, but Alex could tell there was something worth trying for between them. "Because I'm not her."

"That only makes it worse," Megan said. "It would be like adding one more casualty to the tally."

"You know not all breakups have to be ugly, right?" Alex asked. Then with a laugh, she tried to lighten the mood. "And you know we're not officially dating, right? It's like you're running through our eventual breakup before we're even together."

"Let's just say that I don't trust myself when it comes to heartbreak," Megan said. "Can we leave it at that?"

"For now," Alex said. "You want dessert?"

They ordered coffee and slices of pie—cherry for Alex, peach crumble for Megan—and while they watched their waitress go over to the dessert case beside the cash registers and serve up their selections, they fell back into easy conversation. Alex resisted the urge to tell Megan about the goopy mess of freeze-dried survival food that the Home Shopping Network considered a peach cobbler, but she did entertain her with a list of the top ten most ridiculous things her mother had purchased in the last year (*Glitter hair stamps. Ceramic clown figurines. Squatty potty.*). If she couldn't laugh about it, then surely she'd cry.

While they ate their pie, Megan said, "How about we make a deal?"

"What kind of deal?" Alex asked.

"You're right about the friendship thing," Megan answered. "It's not going to work. We're both far too hot and amazing to maintain a platonic relationship. But I don't know if either one of us is really relationship material at this point in time."

"I guess that's fair," Alex said. She didn't really like where Megan was headed, but at least she wasn't suggesting that they never see each other again, which was what she'd been afraid of after their coffee shop date. "What do you propose?"

"I think we should just keep doing what we've been doing," Megan said. "Texting, meeting up when our schedules are free—just light and flirty. We'll go slow for you, and casual for me."

"Well, I don't know about light," Alex said. "We're both kind of dark and twisty people, it seems."

"You're right," Megan said with a laugh, and then she reached across the table to take Alex's hand, kissing the back of it and shooting her a smile that sent sudden desire between Alex's thighs.

NINETEEN

Alex could still feel Megan's electricity running through her when she got home. She couldn't remember the last time she laughed and enjoyed herself like that, let alone the last time she felt this way about a girl. The last time she was carefree enough to have a day like this would have been freshman year of college, and that seemed like a lifetime ago. There was something unique about Megan, and the way she made Alex feel. Whenever they were in a room together, everything else seemed to fade away—everything except Megan was unimportant, and Alex liked that feeling very much.

When she went into her house, she found it oddly silent.

It was the first time in ages that the Home Shopping Network wasn't droning from the living room. She peeked her head in and found the couch empty, and for a second, Alex felt her heart drop into her stomach. Her first thought was that her mother must be sick, or hurt.

For over a year, she hadn't moved from the couch except to go to the bathroom, the kitchen, or bed, and even then she liked to use the smaller television on her dresser as a white noise machine.

Then Alex saw a note addressed to her on the coffee table. She picked it up.

> *Went to the post office, be back around five. Call my*
> *cell if you want me to pick up anything for dinner.*
> *Mom*

Alex didn't know what to make of this at first—it was such a mundane thing to say, so *normal* after more than twelve months of arrested development. Her mother was at the post office and she was going to pick up dinner. *Huh.* After a moment of contemplation, Alex set the note down where she'd found it and went into her room. It was a big step forward for her mom, and Alex was glad that the talk they had the other night appeared to have done some good.

She closed her bedroom door and collapsed onto the bed with a sigh. She let her thoughts run back to Megan, and to their conversation at the diner. Alex hadn't laughed so hard in years, and even though it was the kind of laughter that danced on the edge of tears, threatening to spill over if the wrong word was said, it felt good.

It felt nice to have her emotions back, and to be experiencing such pleasurable ones thanks to Megan. Alex thought about the call room, and how nice it had been to feel close to someone, even if she knew the pills were keeping her at arm's length from the world.

She'd been tapering off them for a little while, though, and she wondered if she'd gotten enough of the meds out of her system yet. The house would be empty for at least another twenty minutes by the time her mother fought through the rush hour traffic.

She rolled onto her stomach and slid one hand under the waistband of her jeans, closing her eyes and bringing up the image of Megan's face, her green eyes, those plump lips, the curves of her body. Alex moved her hips up and down against her hand and imagined what it would be like to make love to her. Even the thought made her blush after so long suppressing those feelings, but she persisted.

She pictured Megan laying in the bed with her, their limbs entwined and their bodies moving together. She imagined what it would feel like to slowly undress her, savoring every inch of flesh as she peeled Megan's clothes away. She recalled the softness of Megan's lips, and—rubbing her fingers more urgently against herself—she remembered the way Megan's mouth had closed around her and her tongue had glided softly over her.

Alex imagined doing the same to Megan, sliding down to the end of the bed and hooking her arms beneath Megan's knees to bury her face between her thighs. With the thought of sliding her fingers through Megan's wetness, Alex turned her face to moan into the bedsheets and continued to move her hips in time with her fantasy.

She'd stay between Megan's thighs as long as she

could—days, weeks, if that's what she wanted—and when she was satisfied, Alex would wrap her arms around Megan, guiding her hand between her legs.

Alex pressed her face more firmly into the sheets, her hips moving insistently against her palm. She replayed the image of Megan's hand sliding between her legs again and again in her mind, and she kept moving her hips even though she was beginning to feel out of breath. She was so close, just a few strokes away from climax, and yet it kept evading her.

When she heard the garage door opening in the distance, Alex pulled her hand away and muttered into the sheets, "*Fuck*."

Breathing heavy and feeling frustrated, she went into the bathroom to wash up and look at herself in the mirror, brushing the wrinkles out of her clothes and running a comb through her hair. The pills clearly hadn't worn off yet, and as she went to greet her mother, she tried to push away the nagging fear that she might have lost that part of her forever.

TWENTY

Megan felt conflicted after the day she spent with Alex, swabbing teenagers and getting to know her in the diner. It had been a fantastic day, perfectly balanced between medicine and flirtation, but she wondered what impression she'd left Alex with when they parted. Megan had told her that they would go slow and keep things casual, but she wasn't sure if that was a promise she could keep.

How could they go slow and have days like that without developing feelings for each other? And how could they keep things casual while still going slow? It was a contradiction in terms, and the more Megan thought about it, the more clear it became that the two of them were looking for very different things. She didn't know how to reconcile that, and she also knew that she'd become too invested in Alex to just walk away.

After all, they'd agreed to be friends and that had only lasted a few days before it was clear that friendship was not on the table. But neither was anything else, between Megan's demanding schedule, her determination not to open her heart to the possibility of a relationship, and Alex's need to go slow and ease back into the world.

Megan went to bed that night with a stupid grin on her face, thinking about how much fun she'd had with Alex and pushing away the doubts and reservations she felt as she closed her eyes and drifted into dreams of chestnut-haired beauties with soft lips and laughs that made Megan's heart leap for joy.

SHE WAS JUST LAYING Alex down on her bed, gently guiding her onto the mattress and holding her close, when she heard her bedroom door creak open behind her. Because Megan's dream self was just as pragmatic as she was in her waking life, she called over her shoulder, "Chloe, a little privacy please," and kept her eyes locked on Alex.

She waited impatiently for the door to click shut again —Chloe had never invaded her space before, it was so unlike her—but Megan didn't hear the latch, and Alex was beginning to look alarmed. Her eyes were fixed on a point over Megan's shoulder, and she was curling up on the bed, drawing her knees protectively to her chest.

"What's wrong?" Megan asked her, but before Alex could answer, she heard the sobbing behind her.

Megan turned around and saw Ruby, or rather, a

grotesque nightmare version of her ex-girlfriend. Where in real life she was tall and athletic, her smooth skin and curly hair her best features, now she was gaunt and frail-looking. Her hair looked brittle and unwashed, her cheeks were sunken like she'd been starving, and mascara streaked down her cheeks in long black rivers.

"This is what you did to me," Ruby said, her voice wavering as she spoke. "This is what I became after you destroyed me."

"I didn't mean to," Megan said, her excuse sounding weak even to her own ears. "I was just scared—"

"I was scared, too," Ruby screeched, making Megan and Alex both wince, and then suddenly her hand shot out, reaching for Megan.

She felt her heart stop momentarily in her chest and she stepped back, out of Ruby's reach. When her pulse caught up to her, she felt silly for the terror that had flooded her in that moment. She'd been with Ruby for six years, and they were friends all through elementary school before that. And now she was afraid of her just because of a little streaky mascara and sunken cheeks?

"I know I hurt you," Megan said, changing her tactic. She glanced down at Alex, who was staring wide-eyed from Megan to Ruby and back again, and knew she had to diffuse this situation. "Ru-Ru, I'm sorry. I could see the end of our relationship looming and I thought it would be less painful if it ended abruptly, no lingering or trying to make things work. I didn't have the courage to stick around and do it the right way, and I'm sorry that I hurt you."

Tears were streaming down her own cheeks now, and the next time that Ruby swung her arm out, making a swipe for the front of Megan's shirt, she stepped backward again and tripped on the bed, falling backward onto the mattress with a yelp. She scrambled up to the head of the bed, where Alex was still curled up, and tried to put her arms around her.

"No," Alex said, pushing Megan away. "You're not doing that to me, too."

She crawled off the bed and ducked under Ruby's extended arm, heading straight for the bedroom door and slamming it on her way out. Ruby was sobbing loudly and Megan opened her mouth to scream in frustration—

And she jolted awake, her sheets wet with perspiration and her bedroom dark. It was the middle of the night, and it took her a moment to orient herself in her room, alone in bed. What she'd done to Ruby was never going to stop haunting her.

FOR THE NEXT FEW WEEKS, though, Megan and Alex were true to their word. Despite all the things weighing on Megan's mind about why their arrangement couldn't work, she managed to keep things light and casual. The fact that they both had busy class schedules probably helped, meaning that the majority of their interactions took place through text messages during the day.

They got coffee or a quick meal in between classes sometimes, and once they'd attempted to study together.

Alex suggested it, saying that since they both had a lot of studying to do every night they could make their own little study group, and they'd met at the café with their backpacks full of homework. That was the first and only time they tried to study together, because they started by chatting over coffee, and four hours later they were still talking and neither one of them had taken so much as a textbook out of their backpacks.

So they set boundaries, resisting the urge to text each other at certain hours that they'd designated as study times. Megan was dead serious about maintaining her class rank and keeping it higher than Ivy's, and Alex had a lot of memorizing and practicing to do if she was going to pass her EMT certification exam in just a few short months.

And in all the free moments of her day, Megan thought about Alex. She either thought about her, or thought about how she really ought not to be thinking so much about that girl. It scared her how close they were getting, how much Alex knew about her and how much Megan looked forward to their time together.

Then one day in late October, Megan came back to the apartment after class to find Chloe sitting on the couch and pouting.

"Hey Chlo," Megan said as she came in and tossed her backpack on the floor by the door. "Whatcha doing?"

"Looking at airfare prices," she said with a sigh. "It's almost not worth going home for Thanksgiving, espe- cially when all I get for a four hundred-dollar flight is a couple days of my relatives asking me when I'm going to find a husband."

Megan let out an involuntary snort, then asked with a little more sympathy, "You're not out to your family yet?"

"Sort of. I'm out to my immediate family, but I can't really expect my eighty-year-old nana to remember I like girls instead of boys, and it seems like an awkward thing to announce to the aunts and uncles I only see a few times a year," Chloe said. She seemed more serious than usual, her tone lacking its usual chipper quality, and it was no fun to tease her when she was upset, so Megan sat down on the couch to lend a sympathetic ear instead. Chloe said, "It would be so much easier if I had a girl-friend to bring home, though. More fun, too."

She glanced up at Megan, and was that a slight raise of her eyebrows as they locked eyes?

"And more money for the flight," Megan pointed out.

"That's true," Chloe said, closing her laptop and putting it on the coffee table. With a sigh, she added, "It's like they forget that I'm in med school, like I'm nothing more than a single woman, and all they can focus on is when I'm going to *find a nice man*. What about you? Does your family bug you about being single at the holidays?"

"Well, my little brother bugs me in general," Megan said, laughing. "But I guess my parents would be happy if I settled down."

She thought about Alex, and for the first time she wondered if Alex had told her mother about her. In Alex's head, were they dating? They certainly hadn't had that talk, but Megan could admit that it was a weird situation to try to explain—more than friends, less than girlfriends, and sadly, not lovers. Megan had chosen to deal with the issue by avoiding it—she hadn't brought Alex to the apartment, Chloe didn't know about her, and her parents definitely didn't know about her. The only person who knew was Ivy, and that was only because she was such a nosy jerk.

"We should just pretend to date until the holidays are over," Chloe said with a sigh, and then she put her hand on top of Megan's on the couch cushion between them.

It caught Megan off-guard, and for a moment she was speechless. Ever since Chloe moved in, Megan had been trying to decide if she had a crush on her—she was always so complimentary, and so helpful, and sometimes it seemed like she'd do anything for Megan, like baby her when she woke up with a migraine. But Chloe was so bubbly and enthusiastic about everyone and everything— hell, she even liked *Ivy*—and Megan could never be certain if she really was getting special treatment. Now, there didn't seem to be much doubt about it.

"Whoa," she said, gently slipping her hand out from under Chloe's. She decided to approach this situation the way she approached most tricky things—with humor. "You know I don't date—even if it's make-believe."

Clouds formed behind Chloe's sky-blue eyes for a moment, and then she perked up, patted Megan's hand again as if that action would wipe away the earnestness of the previous one, and then she said, "I know, silly. It was a joke."

"Good one," Megan said. "You got me."

She got up from the couch, all too eager to extract herself from that moment, and went into the kitchen to retrieve a bottle of juice from the refrigerator. While she was pouring it into a glass, Chloe called from the couch, "You know you're going to have to get back out there eventually."

"What's that supposed to mean?" Megan asked.

"We've been living together for over a year and I've never seen you go on a single date," Chloe said.

That was true, but it wasn't the whole story—Megan had her fair share of hook-ups last year, but it felt wrong to broadcast it to Chloe so she'd always just said she was going to the library to study. It was true enough of the time—the library was practically Megan's second home—but it was also a handy excuse, which she'd continued to use without thinking twice whenever she was going out to meet Alex.

"I know you think your ex-girlfriend damaged you forever," Chloe said—to which Megan answered in her mind, *the opposite actually*—and then she added, "You're never going to get over her if you don't tear down the walls you put up around yourself."

"It's not that," Megan said, then she shook her head sadly and tried to maintain a sympathetic face as she said, "I just happen to find you annoying."

"Shut up," Chloe said, grabbing the nearest throw pillow off the couch and hurling it in Megan's direction.

She missed, Megan blew her a kiss, and said in a

voice that imitated Chloe's own cheerful tone, "Love you."

"Love you too, you stone-hearted bitch," Chloe said with a roll of her eyes, and then Megan headed down the hall to her room.

TWENTY-ONE

As the leaves began to fall with greater speed and the weather turned colder, Megan and Alex continued to find time to see each other whenever they could in the midst of their busy schedules. Usually this involved the cafes and diners around Evanston, and sometimes it involved a quiet corner booth where no one would see them leaning in to pay more attention to each other than their meals.

They kissed, held hands, and Megan ate the majority of the meals they enjoyed together with one arm slung around Alex's shoulder. It felt a lot like being a teenager again, dipping their toes slowly into the waters of sexuality, and it was fun, but it was also frustrating as hell. All Megan wanted to do most nights was kiss Alex deeply, press her body against Alex's curves, smell her, taste her, give her pleasure and feel the way her own body was aching to respond.

And of course, they teased each other and texted each other daily. Megan loved Alex's witty replies, and she found herself reaching for her phone all the time, craving more of her. They talked about everything from their classwork to their future plans. They flirted and told each other about their days. One evening when Megan was supposed to be studying, she heard her phone vibrate and she couldn't resist the urge to pick it up. She was rewarded with a text from Alex.

I came home tonight to find my mom washing the dishes.

Megan remembered the things that Alex had told her about her mother, and how hard she'd taken the loss of her husband. This was a good sign, and Megan answered back with a joking, *Moms Gone Wild.*

It sounds like such a small thing, but for her it's a big deal.

I can count on one hand the number of times she's been in the kitchen over the past year.

Megan smiled, and answered, *That's good. I guess she's moving on, too.* Alex didn't answer back right away, and Megan wondered if she'd inadvertently pushed Alex too far. But then the answer came.

Yeah. I mean, she went right back to the television when she was done, but it's a step. At least she's trying.

We're both trying.

Megan smiled again at this, and then she put the phone face-down on her desk. It was study time, and if she was going to make this work with Alex, whatever it was they were doing, then she'd have to learn to segment her life in order to keep up with her classes.

ONE AFTERNOON IN NOVEMBER, Megan met Alex at a movie theater not far from campus. She was wearing a plaid dress under a fleece jacket. It was perfect for the changing season but which, to Megan's unanswered desires, looked like nothing more than a long shirt that grazed the middles of Alex's thighs.

"You look hot," Megan growled the moment they met on the sidewalk. She put one hand on Alex's hip as they kissed, and it was hard to resist the urge to let it slide lower, to the hem of her dress.

But then Alex stepped away, taking Megan's hand and pulling her over to the ticket counter. "Come on, we don't have much time before the movie starts."

"Please tell me you're not one of those people who likes to watch all the previews," Megan said. The wind picked up Alex's long, thick hair and Megan could smell the lavender on her skin. She wanted to melt into her, and she squeezed Alex's hand a little tighter to signal her desire. It had been over a month now, and she'd had about enough of the slow stuff.

"I am," Alex answered, "and I'm going to answer all the trivia, too."

"Nerd," Megan managed to shoot back, but all of her attention was on the intense way that she was craving Alex today. They'd done it Alex's way long enough, and Megan had compromised for her, but she didn't know how much more she could take of this exquisite torture—especially if she was going to wear a dress like *that*.

They went into the almost empty theater. It was a late afternoon showing and they had their pick of seats. Megan led Alex to the back of the theater, sitting in the very last row.

"Best seats in the house," she said, then glanced over at Alex. "Can you read your precious trivia questions from back here?"

"Yep," Alex said. "This is perfect."

She slid her hand into Megan's, threading their fingers together and resting the back of her hand against Megan's thigh. It was the most intimate thing that Alex had done thus far, and Megan was becoming more and more certain that her choice of dress was intentional. The fabric had inched slightly higher on Alex's leg when she sat down, and Megan spared a quick glance at the softness of her thigh, wondering whether Alex would object if she put her hand on the bare skin there.

"Ellen," Alex said, and Megan was taken aback.

"What?"

Alex just laughed and nodded at the screen, where a trivia question asked, *In the 2003 animated film,* Finding Nemo, *who voiced Dory?*

"Oh," Megan said with a laugh, rubbing her thumb over Alex's hand. "Sheesh, I thought you were sitting there thinking about another woman."

"I wouldn't dream of it," Alex said with a smile, and Megan leaned over the arm rest between them to kiss her. A few more trivia questions marched by on the screen without acknowledgement by the time they finally broke their kiss and Alex said, "I wanted to tell you something."

"Is it that you'd rather be here with Ellen?"

"I guess if the opportunity arose I wouldn't pass it up," Alex admitted with a laugh.

"I don't blame you," Megan answered. Most of the time she could look into those steely eyes all day, but right now she only wanted to pull Alex into another kiss. She resisted, though, and waited for Alex to finish her thought.

"I'm done tapering," she said, and for the first time tonight, Megan caught a glint of desire in her eyes, too. It sent a shiver of anticipation through her—was Alex saying what Megan thought she was saying? She amended, "Well, technically I finished with the pills a week ago, but they're out of my system now, and so are all the negative side effects."

"Wow," Megan said. "That's great. How are you feeling?"

"I feel good," Alex said, her voice indicating that she

was a little surprised by this. "It's nice to be my old self again."

Megan put her hand on the back of Alex's head, pulling her close so that she could kiss her forehead, and then the lights began to dim around them. Alex nudged Megan, bringing their lips to meet, and as the first preview began to play, she opened her mouth and slipped her tongue between Megan's lips.

TWENTY-TWO

When the movie was over and the lights went back up, there was no doubt about what Megan and Alex both wanted next. Alex could feel her breath getting caught in her throat every time her thoughts strayed from the silver screen to her hand on Megan's thigh. They'd gotten off to a rocky start, but then Megan had been so patient and understanding for the last few weeks, and now Alex was finally ready to take their relationship to the next level.

They walked out of the theater and stood for a moment on the sidewalk, neither one of them wanting to voice their desires for fear that the other wouldn't reciprocate, and Alex was gratefully when, finally, Megan said, "My apartment's not far from here. Do you want to come over for a little while?"

"Yeah," Alex agreed, reluctantly letting her hand fall from Megan's as they went over to Megan's car parked on the street.

"There's not much street parking by my place, and the lot is for residents only," Megan said apologetically. "I'll drive you back to your car later if that's okay."

"Sure," Alex said, and the moment she was alone in the car with Megan, the tension between them became palpable. She wondered which one of them would break first, lunging across the center console toward the other, but they both managed to behave, talking in an uncharacteristically stilted manner about the movie while Megan drove the short distance to her apartment. It turned out to be about four blocks away, which was good because Alex didn't think she could handle the suspense of a longer drive.

"It's mostly undergrads who live here," Megan explained as they walked up the stairwell to the third floor. "I could have lived in one of the graduate dorms on campus, but I had such a good lease here that it was cheaper to stay, especially after I found Chloe to take the other bedroom."

"I lived on campus when I was a freshman at the University of Illinois, in a triple room with two girls I didn't know and who owned entirely too much stuff," Alex said, laughing. "We were packed in there like sardines and the walls were paper-thin."

"Dorm living at its finest," Megan said. Megan unlocked the door on the right. "Here we are, home sweet home."

She went in first, clicking on a floor lamp near the door that cast the room in a warm glow, and Alex followed, closing the door behind her. The apartment was bigger than she expected, and well-decorated with a plush, inviting sofa in the middle of the living area and a meticulously clean kitchen along one wall.

"What do you think?" Megan asked, shrugging off her jacket and hanging it on a hook near the door, then coming over to Alex to help her do the same.

As Megan put her hands on Alex's shoulders, tugging off her fleece jacket, Alex smiled at the warmth this gesture created along every point of contact from her shoulders to her wrists. Megan hung up her jacket and Alex turned to face her, smiling as she teased, "It's cleaner than I expected for a med student."

"What's that supposed to mean?" Megan asked.

"I don't know," Alex said. "I just kind of pictured you as one of those people who are highly organized when it comes to your studies but neglects everything else. An Einstein type."

"Well, I'll take the Einstein compliment, I guess," Megan said. "But stereotype much?"

Alex laughed and said, "Fair enough. I got that one wrong."

"Actually, this is my roommate's doing. She's a clean freak," Megan said, and Alex laughed as she added, "You should see the state of my room."

"I knew it," Alex said with a wry smile. Then she asked, "So where is your roommate, anyway?"

"Study group," Megan said. "They meet every week, and it usually lasts for hours. Sometimes days."

Megan stepped a little closer, putting her hands on Alex's hips, and Alex asked, "Days?"

A laugh began to bubble up in her throat, but before it had a chance to come out, Megan kissed her. Alex allowed her body to melt into Megan's with only a little trepidation. The medication would be out of her system now, but she still wasn't totally sure how her body would respond to Megan, or for that matter, how her heart would respond.

Her pulse was pounding in her ears as she pulled away from Megan ever so slightly, just enough to murmur, "Do you want to show me your messy bedroom?"

Megan licked her lips, and then growled, "So badly."

She took Alex's hand and guided her silently, almost solemnly, down the hall. She pushed open a door, revealing a sparsely decorated room with a bed in one corner and a desk full of textbooks and medical journals in another. Megan stepped aside and let Alex enter, and she took stock of the space for a moment, willing her heart rate to settle before they continued.

The bed had about a dozen pillows strewn all over it, and to the right of the desk there was a small bookshelf packed with a surprising number of pulp fiction romances. She cocked an eyebrow at Megan when she saw them—Alex hadn't taken her for a romance reader—but she didn't tease her about them. Instead, she headed back to Megan's side and said, "Not as messy as I was expecting."

"Thanks," Megan said. "I'll take that as a compliment."

Then she wrapped her arms around Alex's waist and squeezed, just tight enough for Alex to know that the gesture was one of ownership. It sent a thrill through her, and she put her arms around Megan's neck, pulling her into a kiss. They stood in the center of the room for a few minutes longer, their tongues dancing in each other's mouths and their bodies inching closer and closer, and then Alex started walking backward to the bed, pulling Megan with her.

When they got there, Alex's calves pressing up against the mattress, Megan paused and asked quietly, "Are you sure you're ready?"

"Yes," Alex said, and the anticipation she felt was intense, as if this were her first time, instead of just her first time in a long while. She knew for certain that she wanted it though—she wanted Megan.

She sat down on the bed, her hands still on the back of Megan's neck and pulling her down to join her. Alex scooted further back onto the bed, kicking her shoes off in the process and watching eagerly as Megan crawled onto the mattress with her and took off her own shoes. She carefully guided Alex onto her back, shoving the excess of pillows away and letting a few of them fall onto the floor as she settled beside Alex and they kissed again.

Megan put one hand on Alex's side, running her palm up and down over the soft plaid of her dress, and just as her thumb brushed over the side of Alex's breast,

CARA MALONE

she paused one more time to say, "Just let me know if it's too much."

"Put your hands on me," Alex begged, taking Megan's hand and holding it firmly against her breast. It was nice of Megan to be so cautious, but they'd been teasing each other for hours—weeks if she counted all of the tense moments in coffee shops and library stacks and hospital call rooms—and she just wanted this moment to come.

Thankfully, Megan didn't need any further encouragement. She squeezed Alex's curves in her hands, running her thumbs over her nipples through several layers of fabric and only managing to increase Alex's sense of urgency. She could feel her body coming back to life, responding in all the right ways to Megan's touch, and she felt relief.

They undressed each other, pausing with each new bit of exposed skin to taste and kiss each other. Alex's hands found the clasp of Megan's bra, popping it open and pulling the straps down over her shoulders as Megan shimmied out of it, and Alex put her hands on her. Her skin was warm and soft, her curves inviting under Alex's hands, just as she had imagined.

"You're beautiful," Alex whispered, her whole body already on fire and goosebumps standing up all over her skin. She wasn't cold—she was electrified in Megan's presence.

Megan kissed Alex, her tongue swirling briefly through her mouth, and then as she kissed her way down Alex's neck, she murmured into her skin, like a secret she was whispering to Alex's body, "So are you."

Her lips inched down over Alex's chest, taking lengthy detours over each of her breasts, learning the contours of her curves. She traced a finger down the center of Alex's stomach and then, skipping over her panties, ran her hand along the inside of Alex's thigh.

She kissed Alex just above the tiny satin bow stitched to the waistband of her underwear, and her breath was hot against Alex's skin. Her fingers played at the elastic and teased her while Alex craved Megan's touch. She just wanted to arch her hips, bring them up to meet Megan's body, but instead she waited patiently, running her hands through Megan's wild hair and closing her eyes in anticipation.

She felt Megan's fingers hook under the waistband of her panties, and Alex raised her hips to help her pull them down. Then Megan's hands were on her legs, and her lips were kissing a trail up from her knee to the inside of her thighs. Her breath caught as Megan's mouth found her, and her tongue glided through the wetness between her legs.

They moaned in unison the moment her tongue made contact, and Alex reached down to take Megan's hand from where it lay on her stomach. It felt every bit as good as she'd been hoping for, and Alex relaxed, enjoying the sensations of Megan's lips and tongue as they explored every inch of her and made her body fill with tingling, hot desire.

After a minute of slow, teasing licks, Megan slid a finger between Alex's thighs, moving in and out of her wetness and ratcheting up the pleasurable sensations that washed over Alex with every thrust and swipe. She moved her hips in rhythm with Megan's movements and pulled one of Megan's numerous pillows over her face, sighing and moaning into it as Megan brought her closer to the edge.

All of her fears and insecurities faded away, along with every other thought in her mind, and Alex focused entirely on the way Megan was making her feel. She wanted to live in this moment forever, and she wanted to commit every stroke and every lick to memory. Before long, Megan had her teetering on the edge, squeezing her eyes shut and letting out a tortured moan into the pillow before finally, she felt relief wash over her and her thighs shivered against Megan's shoulders as she climaxed.

ALEX AND MEGAN laid together in her bed after they'd both been satisfied, neither one of them willing to leave that moment. Megan leaned over the edge of the bed and snatched a couple of pillows off the floor. They were both still breathing heavily, their hair wet with sweat and their bodies still thrumming out the rhythm of their pleasure. Megan tucked one of the pillows under Alex's head, but she didn't use it. Instead, Alex wanted to be as close to her as possible, nestling her head into the crook of Megan's arm and enjoying the rise and fall of Megan's breathing.

"So, was that okay?" Megan asked, kissing the top of

Alex's head and pulling one of her many blankets on top of them when Alex began to shiver from the cool air in the room.

Alex looked up at her, and she couldn't decide whether to come up with something snarky or just be honest for once. The truth was that she had no words for how good it had felt to be with Megan—not just because she'd given Alex her first orgasm in over a year. She'd also given her the courage to go on with her life after an extended mourning period. In the end, Alex decided on the honest answer, saying, "That's the best I've felt in a long time."

"Good," Megan said, giving her a quick kiss and then grinning. "But to be more explicit, the sex was incredible, right? That had to be the most mind-blowing orgasm you've ever had, right?"

Alex laughed and playfully pushed Megan. She was grateful to her for always knowing when to lighten the mood with her unique brand of bragging humor. Alex said, "It was a solid top five performance."

"Top *five*?" Megan exclaimed. "I'm offended."

Alex laughed and said, "Oh please, I know you like a challenge. You're so competitive, I bet you'll take every opportunity to climb the ranks."

"Challenge accepted," Megan said, wrapping her arms tighter around Alex. She kissed her, and before long, her mouth was beginning to stray lower, over Alex's jaw and then down her neck. Megan flipped the blanket up over her head and kissed a line down over Alex's stomach, and Alex closed her eyes again, focusing on the sensations coming from beneath the covers. This was the most peaceful she had felt in a long time, and it wasn't just the physical release. There was something comforting about Megan, and Alex wondered if this was what falling in love felt like.

TWENTY-THREE

Megan realized only when she heard her phone vibrating that she'd dozed off. She had laid down next to Alex, arms wrapped around her, and closed her eyes for a moment. Now as she opened them and zeroed in on the source of the noise, she saw that it had gotten dark outside the streetlights had come on outside her window.

She separated herself reluctantly from Alex, who was just waking up again too, and Megan wondered how much time had passed. She shivered as she walked naked across the room and dug her phone out of the pocket of her pants, where they'd ended up on the floor. The screen said it was past eight o'clock, and the call she was receiving was from Chloe. Megan glanced longingly back at Alex, still curled up beneath the blankets and watching her, and she thought about ignoring the call. She'd already pushed aside her responsibilities for most of the afternoon, though, and it was probably time to come back to reality.

Megan answered the call, "Hey Chlo, what's up?"

"I just got out of the study group," Chloe said. "I was going to stop for food on the way home and I just called to see if you'd eaten yet."

"Thanks," Megan said. She hadn't even begun to think of food tonight, having been far too distracted with Alex. "I'm good, but I appreciate it."

"Okay, be home soon," Chloe said, and then she hung up.

"Anything important?" Alex asked from the bed.

"No, just my roommate telling me she's on her way home," Megan said, coming over and leaning on the mattress to give Alex a kiss but resisting the urge to crawl back into bed with her. "I didn't realize how late it had gotten."

"What time is it?" Alex asked as Megan turned on the overhead light and then went back over to the pile of clothes on the floor and picked up her jeans to put them back on. Megan told her, and Alex got out of bed, too. "I should go—my mom's going to be wondering where I am."

Megan handed Alex her dress, then her bra, and finally her panties after she'd found them tangled in the sheets. They both got dressed, stealing shy glances at each other. Tonight's events had far surpassed Megan's expectations and she'd had a lot of fun, but getting dressed in the harsh artificial light, she couldn't help but be reminded that they still hadn't defined their relationship, and that the odds were good that Alex wanted more from it than Megan did. She wondered briefly if she'd made a mistake in letting her desires get the best of her.

She walked Alex back through the living room and kissed her at the door, her mind already turning to the readings she'd need to complete for the next day's lecture, and Alex asked, "I'll talk to you tomorrow?"

"Yeah," Megan said, wondering again if tonight had been a bad idea. It certainly seemed like something had shifted in their dynamic, and she wished there was a way to delicately remind Alex that nothing about their arrangement had changed. She was still too busy for a girlfriend, and too damaged.

Instead, she let her go, and Megan headed back toward her room to start studying.

She didn't make it far—she hadn't even left the living room before the door swung open again, and Megan expected it to be Alex, saying she'd forgotten something. Instead, it was Chloe—they must have passed each other in the stairwell, and Megan wondered with a smirk if either of them realized it.

"Hey," Chloe said, neatly hanging her coat from a hook near the door and setting down her backpack along with a take-out bag on the dining table.

"How was the study group?" Megan asked.

"We did a pretty thorough review of the respiratory system," Chloe said. "You should join us sometime."

"Studying with Satan?" Megan asked. "As much as that sounds like a whimsical YouTube channel, I think I'll pass."

"Ivy's not Satan," Chloe chastised, going over to the kitchen to get a plate. "She's just really focused on her school work and determined to be the best doctor she can be."

"I just wish she didn't have to step on *my* back to get there," Megan said. She could never see the good in Ivy the way that Chloe did. Then again, Chloe could see the good in a big, hairy spider scuttling across their floor, so her opinion didn't count for much. Chloe sat down at the table, taking a burger and fries out of the take-out bag, and Megan snatched one of the fries off her plate.

"I thought you said you weren't hungry," Chloe objected.

"I'm not," Megan answered around a mouthful of deep-fried goodness. In truth, she was beginning to feel a little bit peckish, but it was a feeling that was easily ignored—she had too much work to catch up on to worry about food, and Alex was still swimming through her mind. For the second time, she wondered if she might have made a mistake tonight, promising Alex more than she could deliver.

"What did you do tonight?" Chloe asked while she ate, pushing the plate toward Megan to offer her another French fry.

They smelled so good and Megan hadn't eaten since breakfast. Giving in, she sat down and took a couple, then without even really thinking about it, she continued the lie that she'd been feeding Chloe, omitting Alex from her life. "Nothing. Just went to my afternoon lab and then spent the afternoon making progress on my research paper. The end of the module is coming up fast."

That much was true, but Megan had been neglecting her paper, and she knew that getting it done on time would be a photo finish. With a snort, she thought that Ivy had probably already turned hers in, and Megan was willing to bet that Chloe was close to done with hers, too. How could she let a pretty girl distract her so much?

"You should have come to the study session with us," Chloe said again. "We spent about an hour critiquing each other's papers. I bet you would have appreciated that."

If I had anything to critique, Megan thought, a sense of dread settling in her chest. She had a couple of interviews with Dr. Stevens and a loose stack of scholarly articles laying on her desk, but nothing to critique. She really was falling behind.

"Did you end up booking your plane ticket home?" she asked, trying to change the subject in order to clear her conscience.

"Not yet," Chloe said. "I'm thinking about taking a bus. The tickets are way cheaper and there are always such interesting people on the bus."

Megan laughed. *Only Chloe...*

"You can't take a bus," Megan quipped. "Do you want to be murdered, or molested?"

"The bus is not that bad," Chloe said, rolling her eyes. "Besides, what choice do I have if I want to get home and still have money for Christmas presents?"

"You're right," Megan said. "Sacrifices must be made. Just bring a can of mace with you."

Megan made quick work of Chloe's fries, which she didn't complain about as she ate her burger, and then she took her plate over to the dishwasher and Megan stood up from the table. She really should try to get some work done before bed.

"Hey, wait," Chloe said, coming back from the kitchen.

"Yeah?"

"Remember my pretend dating idea?" Chloe asked as she came back over to the table. "Do you think it could work?"

"Pretending to date during the holidays?" Megan asked, furrowing her brow.

"Med school just gets kind of lonely sometimes, don't you think?" Chloe asked. "I know you don't date and I'm annoying, but wouldn't it be nice to come home to someone?"

"Whoa," Megan said, her heart starting to beat a little faster as she realized a moment too late what was happening.

Chloe leaning in abruptly and kissed Megan. She put her hands on Megan's cheeks and planted her lips against her mouth, and a dozen thoughts flashed through Megan's head. Every single one of them had to do with Alex, but the one that was the most prominent—the one that screamed at the forefront of her mind—was that getting involved with Alex, with *anyone* was a bad idea.

And then something ugly reared its head, bringing Megan's hands to Chloe's hips and sinking into the kiss.

"What the hell?"

It felt almost exactly like the dream that Megan had about Ruby. The voice came from the doorway, and when Megan pulled out of the kiss, she saw Alex standing there, her face slack with shock. Megan yanked her hands off Chloe's hips, but it was too little, too late, and Alex had already seen them deep in a kiss. It was like snapping out of a moment of insanity, and Megan was surprised at the taste of Chloe's lip balm on her mouth.

"Alex—"

"Who?" Chloe asked, narrowing her eyes at the source of the interruption. "Is that the paramedic?"

"I got all the way to my car before I realized my keys had fallen out of my pocket," Alex said, her voice stony.

Megan should have gone to her, apologized, or said *anything* to try to explain that stupid, impulsive, and illogical kiss. Instead, she just stood there while Alex marched through the apartment and into her bedroom, refusing to look at Megan along the way. She emerged a minute later, car keys in her hand, and Megan was still glued to the spot where she stood. She'd just done exactly what she'd spent the last few months trying to avoid, and become the monster that she always knew she was. It seemed like an exceptionally cruel act to chase after Alex and beg for forgiveness, so she let her go.

Alex slammed the door, and Chloe looked at Megan with surprise. "What's going on?"

"Fuck," Megan muttered, putting her hand to her forehead as she felt a headache coming on. "I'm sorry."

It was easier to say to Chloe, because she didn't mean anything to Megan—at least not romantically. Megan sighed deeply and went down the hall to shut herself in her room.

TWENTY-FOUR

Alex could barely see the road on her way home—the tears that fell involuntarily down her cheeks were obscuring her vision, and she had to keep blinking them furiously away. She could still feel Megan's hands on her body, and her lips, and she could feel the fireworks that went off all over her body beneath Megan's fingertips. And to balance all of that, there was a sourness forming in her stomach, and she couldn't erase the sight of Megan kissing her roommate.

Alex didn't know who to be angrier at—Megan for being so brutal, or herself for letting it happen. Megan had told her that she wanted to keep things casual, and that she had baggage, but Alex never imagined in all the time they'd spent with each other in the past few months that there was someone else. To discover her the same night that they'd made love so tenderly made Alex want to be sick.

She turned on the stereo, cranking the volume way

up to obscure her tears and her pain, and settled on the angriest rock she could find. It turned out that at this hour, it got pretty angry.

By the time Alex got home, the pit in her stomach had turned into a tight, aching sensation in her chest and she found herself longing for the ability to be numb. The pills were gone, though, so she knew she'd have to sit with this feeling for a while. Alex sat in the driveway for a long time, waiting for the tears to stop so she could dry her cheeks and do a reasonable job of pretending she hadn't just had her heart broken. She got out of the car and let the cold autumn air hit her face, taking away the redness there, and then she went inside.

Her mother was on the couch, glued to the Home Shopping Network as usual. Alex had hoped after the positive steps she'd taken that she'd come home one day soon and find the television turned off, or at least set to a different channel, but it didn't look like today was that day.

Today was *not* a good day.

Alex stood in the living room doorway, leaning her shoulder against it as she said softly, "I thought you were going to give the television a rest tonight so you could get up early and work on job applications tomorrow."

"Look who's talking," her mother said, reading the time from the bottom corner of the television screen where it was always soldiering forward in one-minute increments that promised a never-ending progression of new products. "It's almost ten and you're just getting home?"

Alex didn't realize it was so late. She shrugged and said, "Yeah, I guess so."

"Don't you have class in the morning?" Her mother asked, and it took Alex a little off-guard. This was the first time that her mom had taken an interested in Alex's education beyond repeatedly suggesting that she should go back to the University of Illinois.

"I do," she said.

"Get some rest then, baby girl," her mom answered. "You want to be fresh for class."

"Yeah," Alex agreed, but instead of leaving, she came over and sat down on the couch.

Even if she went to bed, there would be no sleep for her right now. She put her head down on the arm of the couch, propping it with one of the half-dozen throw pillows that had come from none other than her mother's television family, and watched the host trying desperately to make the Slap Chop seem like an exciting product.

"These pillows are comfy," she said.

"That's the Juneau," her mother said. "Three-hundred thread count, machine-washable slip cover with polyester filling."

"Have you ever considered sending your resume to the Home Shopping Network?" Alex asked, and it was only half in jest. "I bet you'd be ten times more compelling than these people."

She gestured at the television where the host's face was etched permanently into a somewhat unnatural grin.

"I kind of like them that way," her mom said.

"Reptilian?"

"Frozen," her mom answered. "No matter what, you can always count on them to be the same as they were yesterday, and the day before, and the day before."

Alex sat up and looked at her mother—really *looked* at her—for the first time since her dad's funeral. She understood now why her mother had turned his hang-out spot in the garage into a shrine to consumerism, and why she'd blown so much of his life insurance payout on garbage she was never going to use. Alex leaned over and wrapped her arms around her mother's shoulders, giving her a long hug.

She expected her to fight it, to ask Alex what she was doing and why she was making such a fuss over her, but instead, her mom just returned the hug, resting her chin on Alex's shoulder. After a few seconds, she said, "I tried to go to the grocery store today."

"Oh yeah?"

"It didn't go well."

Alex waited a minute, expecting her mom to volunteer more information, and when she didn't, she pulled out of the hug and asked gently, "What happened?"

"I forgot that the park is on the way to the store," she said. "It was like my brain and my hands were no longer communicating, and as much as I wanted to just drive past it and buy some damned bread and milk, I went into the park instead."

Tears brimmed in her eyes as she spoke.

"I parked where we always used to, at the end of the lot under that big, shady oak tree," she said. "And I went to the gazebo where your dad proposed to me. There were people sitting nearby, drinking coffee and holding each other to keep away the cold, and I just stood there for I don't even know how long, letting it chill me to the bone. Finally, someone came up and asked me if I was okay—I think they thought I was a vagrant or something, and I guess I can't blame them."

She gestured to her pants, the same ratty sweats that she'd been rotating through all year and which were now so threadbare that the seams were fraying.

"I got back in the car and came home, and I could feel this great well of sadness threatening to rise up and choke me," she said. "So I sat down and turned on the television, and it all just kind of receded, like floodwater after the rain stops."

Alex leaned over and kissed her mom on the cheek, then sat back up and said, "You tried. It's great that you tried."

"I don't know how you do it, baby girl," she said.

"Not very well," Alex admitted.

She took a deep breath and told her mom about what happened tonight.

"You know that girl I've been hanging out with?" Alex asked. Love and butterflies and girl troubles seemed like such frivolous things when her mom couldn't even get off the couch because of her grieving, and Alex had been telling her mother that she and Megan were just friends. She wondered if this conversation would have been easier if she'd been honest about her feelings all along, to everyone involved.

"Megan," her mom supplied.

"Yeah," Alex said. "Well, we went on a date today and it was so perfect."

She blushed, wondering how much of the details she could tell her mother—they were close, but not 'sharing the details of her sex life' close. In the end she settled on telling her mom only that they'd slept together, and that she'd walked in on Megan kissing her roommate no more than fifteen minutes later.

"She was like a different person," Alex said, looking at the coffee table because she didn't want to start crying again. "She just stood there and waited for me to get my keys, like I was inconveniencing her. It was so humiliating."

"Oh baby," her mother said, pulling Alex into another hug. "People are assholes."

"Yeah," Alex said, then shut her mouth because she could feel the tears threatening the back of her throat.

"You can't let them get to you," she continued. "Everyone's got their own struggles, and sometimes they hurt you without even thinking about it."

"It's just so frustrating," Alex said, not sure if she wanted to punch the Juneau pillow or burst into tears. "She's been keeping me at arm's length ever since we met and I *know* we would have been good for each other if she had just let me in."

"You know better than most how painful that can be," her mom said.

"Too painful," Alex said, sitting up again. "I don't know why I thought I was ready to get off my medication."

"Because you're strong, baby," her mom said. "Lord knows you're stronger than me."

"I don't know if I can do this," Alex said, swiping at an errant tear that was making its way down her cheek. She wanted to be numb, because if she'd been numb, none of this would have happened in the first place.

"You have to do it at your own pace," her mom said sympathetically. "If you're not ready, then maybe you should call the doctor in the morning to talk about restarting the medication."

Alex nodded. The idea of sacrificing her libido for the comfort of numbness didn't sound so bad right now. It wouldn't be much of a sacrifice, because she doubted that she'd ever have another night like this one, anyway.

"You want to order a pizza?" she asked. "I haven't eaten dinner, and I'm willing to bet you haven't, either."

"You're right," her mom admitted.

Alex pulled her phone out of her pocket, momentarily tensing for a message or a missed call from Megan, but there was nothing. Rather than admitting her disappointment, she just dialed the number for their favorite pizza place and pushed the thought away.

WHEN THE PIZZA CAME, Alex tipped the delivery boy generously for coming so late at night and then set the box down on the coffee table, grabbing a few plates and napkins from the kitchen. When she came back, she saw that the television had been switched off.

"Let's talk," her mom said as she noticed Alex looking at the black screen.

"About what?"

"I don't know," she said, reaching for her first slice of pizza. "Whatever you want."

They were silent for a moment while Alex pulled a couple of slices onto her plate and tried to think of conversation topics that didn't involve Megan. She couldn't think any more about her tonight. EMT school was the only other thing in Alex's life right now, but she didn't think her mom would want to hear about performing CPR on a medical dummy.

Finally, though, her mother filled the void.

"We couldn't have ordered this pizza if your dad was still around," she said, surprising Alex. She hadn't voluntarily mentioned him since the funeral, and now she was smiling, a small laugh escaping her lips. "I don't know why he thought green peppers were the devil, but he would never even let me order them on half. He thought they ruined the whole pizza just by being in the same box."

"Yeah," Alex said with a grin, "I remember that. And yet he loved anchovies."

"Your father was a strange man," her mom said with another laugh. It had a strained quality to it, but at least they were talking about him again, and it made the last of Alex's sour stomach fade away. She devoured her pizza, suddenly very hungry.

TWENTY-FIVE

Megan didn't manage to get any work done that night. Instead, she crawled into bed and tried to figure out why the hell she'd allowed that kiss to go on so long, and what had tied her tongue when Alex came back and caught them. She watched as the halogen street lamp burned outside her window and cast her room in a yellow glow, the occasional pedestrian walking by on the sidewalk and sending shadows across her walls, and she didn't have any answers.

Eventually, she heard Chloe getting ready for bed. She heard water running as she brushed her teeth, and finally the click of the door jamb as she went into her room. Megan tried to close her eyes and go to sleep, but she knew there would be no sleep tonight. She didn't really deserve it after how she'd treated both Alex and Chloe. If she could prevent that kiss, she'd do it in a heartbeat. But now that it was done, it seemed like the kinder thing to just let Alex walk away knowing what a monster Megan really was.

If she had chased after her, or if she called her to explain, then Alex might forgive her and open up the possibility for it to happen again. Megan had no idea how she'd lost control of herself so completely—she just knew that fear had bubbled up in her chest when she thought about being there for Alex the way she knew that Alex wanted, and she'd acted out. She couldn't promise that it wouldn't happen again, or that she wouldn't hurt her in an even worse way.

With a groan, Megan gave up on sleep around three a.m. She was exhausted but her mind wouldn't let her get any rest, so she got up and went into the living room—the only thing left to do was inundate herself with late night television. All the news shows were off the air by then, so all she had left to keep her company were infomercials. She turned one on at random, not even caring what the product was, and laid down on the couch. She let her eyes gloss over as she watched. The over-enthusiastic salesman on screen said, "But wait, there's more!" at least once every ten minutes as the night—along with Megan's thoughts—marched on.

THE APARTMENT WAS BRIGHT the next time Megan opened her eyes. She had no memory of closing them, or of dozing off, but the remote control was no longer in her hand and the television had been switched off.

"—class?"

"Huh?" Megan asked, looking over the arm of the couch.

Chloe was standing there with her hair neatly curled and her jacket already on. She said, "I asked if you're coming to class."

"Shit," Megan muttered, sitting up with a feeling of alarm. "What time is it?"

"Quarter til," Chloe said. "You can still make it if you hurry. I'm leaving as soon as the coffee finishes brewing."

"Okay," Megan said, still feeling pretty disoriented. "It's a lecture day, right?"

She could leave with Chloe if she just threw on a pair of jeans and stuffed her laptop into her backpack, but she hated the idea of showing up with greasy hair and no makeup. She could only imagine what Little Miss Perfect —Ivy—would have to say about that. Megan was weighing the consequences of skipping the first hour of class so she could shower.

"Yeah," Chloe said. "But Dr. Morrow mentioned a pop quiz to make sure we're ready for the exam on Friday."

"Damn it," Megan said with a long, frustrated groan, bidding farewell to her hopes of a shower.

She went into her room, yanking down her pajama pants and grabbing the nearest pair of jeans she could find—yesterday's—laying on the floor. As she was buttoning them and hopping toward the closet for a scarf that could cover up her untamed hair, Chloe came and stood in her doorway.

"You're kind of a mess," she said.

"Thanks," Megan answered, ignoring her as she grabbed a sweater off its hanger and pulled it on.

"I didn't say it to be mean," Chloe said as Megan went over to her desk and packed up her laptop and notebooks. "Are you okay?"

"I'm fine," Megan lied, glancing up at Chloe. She looked genuinely concerned, and Megan sighed. "Look, I'm sorry about that kiss—"

"I kissed you," Chloe said, shrugging off the apology. She held out a second travel mug and Megan took it. As they walked back through the living room, Chloe asked, "Was that your girlfriend last night? Did I mess things up between you?"

"God, no," Megan said. "*I* messed things up. You did nothing wrong."

"Okay," Chloe said, and then after a moment of hesitation, she added, "Why did you kiss me back, then?"

"Because I'm a fucking idiot," Megan said, grabbing her coat off the hook by the door. "Can we please stop talking about this?"

"Sure," Chloe said, and they headed out of the apartment.

It was cold out, the late autumn breeze sending a chill through Megan's body, and they walked in silence for a little while as she tried not to think about Alex. It was impossible, but she had to try or else she might as well just skip the class.

As they approached the academic building, Chloe couldn't hold her tongue any more. Megan was surprised that she'd made it as long as she did, but then she asked, "Are you going to apologize to her, too?"

"No," Megan said, trying to make her voice stern enough to shut down any further questions. Of course, she was dealing with Chloe so that would never work.

"Why not?" she demanded.

"It's not worth it," Megan said, trying to convince herself as much as Chloe. "She was just a fling."

"She didn't act like it was a fling," Chloe pointed out.

"I'll kiss you again right now if you stop talking about this," Megan begged, and Chloe was silent again until they reached their seats in the lecture hall.

She sat down beside Megan and they both waved to Ivy when she turned from the front row to look at them— Megan's wave was a bit more sardonic than Chloe's. Then just before Dr. Morrow approached the podium to begin class, she said, "I just hope you're not sabotaging whatever's between you and the paramedic because of that stupid belief you have about damaging people."

"Thanks for the unsolicited advice," Megan said. "I'll keep it in mind."

TWENTY-SIX

Alex tried to forget about Megan over the next few weeks. It was painfully clear by the complete lack of communication on her part that Megan had no further interest in Alex, but it didn't stop Alex from wishing she could have changed the outcome. She knew Megan had the capacity to love her, and that she was acting out of fear that she would somehow hurt Alex, but the irony of what happened seemed completely lost on her.

Alex decided not to call her therapist like her mother suggested. For one thing, she knew the holidays were approaching and there were other patients who needed to see the doctor more than Alex did—people whose problems extended beyond matters of the heart. Besides, in the days after that terrible night, Alex was able to acknowledge that she didn't want to go through the numbness of medication again. She may have stopped taking her anti-depressants because of Megan, but that wasn't the only reason, and Alex's mother was right—she *was* strong enough to get through this. So she decided to push away her feelings for Megan the old fashioned way —with distractions.

She dove into her schoolwork, and discovered a few new bands to fill up the silences. Alex got to be better friends with Sarah, and they spent a lot of time studying together in the evenings, getting ready to take their EMT certification test in January. She also poured a lot of energy into making sure that her mother wasn't falling back into old habits, either. One morning when Alex found her asleep on the couch, a thick fleece blanket wrapped around her and the remote control clenched in her fist, she decided that enough was enough.

"Ma," Alex said as she peeled the remote out of her hand. "Wake up, ma."

"Hmm?"

"Did you fall asleep out here?" Alex asked.

She couldn't remember the last time her mom had done that, not even bothering to get up and brush her teeth before bed. It made Alex's chest feel heavy to see her sleeping there. The truth was that they would *both* be backsliding if they didn't keep their guard up.

"I guess I did," her mom said. Then she added with a shrug, "Oh well, I just would have ended up here again anyway."

She reached for the remote, but Alex held it away from her.

"No, ma," she said. "We can't keep doing this."

She put the remote into the back pocket of her paja-mas, then went over to the front door and stepped into a pair of sneakers that she'd left there the previous night. When she came back into the living room and bent over behind the television, unplugging things, her mom's eyes went wide.

"What are you doing?" she asked.

"What we both should have done a long time ago," Alex said. She picked up the television, slinging the power cord over the top of the screen as she hoisted the whole thing under her arm and added, "And what dad would want us to do."

Her mom didn't object. She just watched from the couch as Alex carried the television outside. She set it down on the curb at the end of the driveway, laying the remote beside it. It might make a good Christmas gift for someone, and she knew it wouldn't last more than an hour out there. When she came back into the house, her mother didn't argue or try to stop her, but she was trembling slightly.

"It's going to be okay, ma," Alex said, and then she went into the kitchen to fix them breakfast.

IT WAS easy to tell herself that she wasn't backsliding during the hours in the day when Alex successfully kept herself busy. It was in the quiet moments that her mind always drifted back to Megan. Her anger faded as the days turned into weeks, and she was left with a profound sense of frustration. Why did Megan have to throw away what they'd been building like that? The more she thought about it, the more Alex was certain it had been a calculated move meant to push her away.

She picked up her phone and opened her old string of text messages with Megan often in those quiet moments, sometimes just to mourn what she'd lost, and other times to wonder what would happen if she reached out to her. It was clear by then that Megan had no intention of contacting Alex, but maybe she could get through to her if they just talked. Inevitably, Alex always put the phone back down again—she had hurt enough, and texting Megan would do nothing but reopen those wounds.

Then one night, Alex was scrolling through those old messages and her mother popped her head into the doorway.

"Hey, baby," she said. "I'm going to make us something for dinner. Spaghetti okay with you?"

"Yeah," Alex said, jumping a little bit and holding the phone down by her side as a guilty streak shot through her. She knew she shouldn't be reading those old messages, torturing herself. She probably should have just deleted the texts and Megan's number along with them, but she didn't want her mother to know what she was doing.

Her mom disappeared down the hall, about to cook her first meal in over a year, and Alex thought she ought to go help her. Before she got that far, though, she heard a faint ringing sound. Looking down at her phone, she realized with horror that she'd accidentally bumped the screen, and she was currently dialing Megan.

Before she could end the call, Megan picked up, and Alex heard her voice coming faintly through the speaker. "Hello?"

"Shit," Alex muttered to herself, her heart rising into her throat as she brought the phone to her ear and said, "Megan?"

"Hey," Megan answered, and she sounded surprised, but not displeased. "What's up?"

"I kind of pocket dialed you," Alex said. "Sorry."

"That's okay," Megan said.

Alex was about to hang up the phone, when instead she asked, "Do you have a minute to talk?"

"Yeah," Megan answered. "Definitely."

"I just feel like things between us ended so abruptly," Alex hurriedly added. "It's just hard to get over something like that without any closure."

"Yeah, I've been having trouble with it, too," Megan admitted, which surprised Alex. "I'm sorry that you saw that kiss."

"You're sorry that I saw it?" Alex asked, incredulous. "What's that supposed to mean? How many others were there before the one that I caught you in?"

"No, no," Megan hurriedly answered. "There were no others. I just meant that I wish it hadn't happened because I know I hurt you."

"Then why did you do it?" Alex demanded.

"I didn't, at first," Megan said. "Chloe kissed me, and I should have pushed her away but instead I let it continue. I kind of lost my mind for a second."

"Bullshit," Alex said. "You're using the insanity defense?"

"Okay, fine," Megan answered. "I was scared."

"*Of what*?"

"I was afraid because you and I were getting closer, and I didn't want it to end the way my first relationship ended," Megan said. "I dated her for a long time and it got to the point where we were only together because it was easier than trying to separate our lives. We lived together, we were in the same sorority–"

"You're a sorority girl?" Alex snorted, unable to help herself.

"Social chair three years running," Megan said with a smirk. "Can you picture it?"

"No," Alex said, shaking her head.

"That's because it's wasn't really my thing. I did it for her," Megan said. "I changed my life in a lot of ways for her, and it was a long time before I realized that I didn't recognize myself anymore. So we broke up."

"I'm sure that was hard, but it happens," Alex said. "That doesn't mean you're responsible for it."

"Oh, I am," Megan said. "It wasn't the fact that we broke up. It was the way I handled it. I basically just shut her out of my life one day because I thought it wouldn't hurt as bad that way. I didn't think about how awful that would be for her."

"So you were trying to protect me by doing the exact same thing?" Alex asked with a sigh.

"Obviously," Megan said with a small laugh. "It sounds pretty stupid when you put it that way."

"It sounds *really* stupid," Alex said. Then after a small pause, she asked tentatively, "So have you learned your lesson?"

"About kissing my roommate and leaving a trail of destruction in my wake?" Megan asked. "I never meant to do any of that. I didn't mean to hurt you, and I don't know how I can promise that it won't happen again."

Alex sighed again and said, "How about you start with not kissing other girls?"

"I can do that, but I can't promise that I'm not going to hurt you in some other way," Megan said.

"I can't promise not to hurt you, either," Alex said. "No one can. Pain is an inevitable part of life."

"I can't do this, Alex," Megan said. "I know that it probably sounds so trivial after what you've gone through, but I can't be broken again. Not now. I'm sorry."

And then the line went dead, and Alex just stared at her phone for a minute, dumbstruck. Had that really just happened? She got up from her desk and went into the kitchen, where her mother was just beginning to boil water in one of the copper pots that came from none other than the Home Shopping Network.

"Can we have spaghetti some other night, ma?" Alex asked.

"Sure, baby," her mother said. "Is everything okay?"

"I would love to get out of the house for a while," Alex answered, and when her mom asked what she had in mind, Alex grinned.

THE SHOPPING MALL that Alex brought her mother to was crowded with people preparing for the upcoming holidays. Alex felt anxious as she drove, and even more so as they went inside—she was taking charge and attempting to draw both of them out of their shells, but really, she had no idea whether this was a good idea or a horrible one.

She drove past the mall that they always used to go to with her father, and instead went a few miles closer to downtown Chicago to the shopping mall that her dad rarely visited. It was a longer drive from the house and it had more expensive shops, but Alex thought the unfamiliarity of the place might help her mom. She'd begun to come back to life after Alex threw away the television, but she still hadn't left the house very many times in the past year, and Alex thought it would be best to ease her into it with the most familiar setting she could find. She watched her as they walked through the crowded corridors and poked their heads tentatively into a few small boutique shops.

"Will you quit it?" her mom snapped about halfway through their second store.

"Quit what?" Alex asked with a frown.

"Quit looking at me like you're Jane Goodall and I'm an ape," she said. "Like you're waiting for me to do something crazy."

"I'm sorry," Alex said, backing up a few paces and giving her mom a little more space. She watched her mom pick up a cashmere scarf hanging on a row of hooks on the wall, running her hand along the soft fabric, and when she saw the price, she laughed and hung it back up.

"They had one just like it on the air last week," she whispered to Alex. "Twenty dollars less."

"Did you buy one?" Alex asked, and her mother huffed.

"No," she said, but then she cracked a smile. "I bought two. Yours is light blue and you're getting it for Christmas."

Alex laughed and breathed a sigh of relief. Her mom seemed to be doing okay after all. They spent about an hour winding their way through the smaller stores, not buying anything. Alex only had her mother to shop for, and her mom had already bought presents for every holiday and gift-giving occasion from now until the apocalypse thanks to the Home Shopping Network.

By the time they got to the big department store at the other end of the mall, they were laughing and joking and having a good time people-watching like they used to do when Alex was a kid. They were walking behind a large family, the mother weighed down with shopping bags and her five kids taking up the whole aisle as they munched on various treats from the food court. For the first time in weeks, Alex didn't feel like she was in a hurry, rushing to get somewhere and find something to distract her, or going to class so she could focus all of her attention there. She felt at peace.

And then one of the kids started choking.

The soft pretzel in his hand fell to the floor and his mom, oblivious thanks to the mayhem of the mall and the wall of shopping bags she carried, just kept walking. The kid turned to one of his older siblings for help, and Alex saw that his lips were a light shade of blue. That's when his mom noticed, turning around and dropping all of her shopping bags as her eyes went wide. She was frozen in shock, but Alex knew exactly what to do.

She turned the kid around and dropped to her knees to get down on his level, then wrapped her arms around him and pumped her fist into his abdomen. His lips turned a darker shade of blue and his mother screeched as Alex tried again. This time a chunk of barely chewed pretzel flew out of his mouth and he started gasping.

Alex let go and stood up, and before she knew what was happening the kid's mom threw her arms around Alex's neck, nearly knocking her backward with the force of her gratitude.

"Thank you," she said as she released Alex from her grip. "Oh my god, I don't know what I would have done if you weren't here."

"Don't worry about it," Alex said, and the woman tried to press a twenty-dollar bill into her palm, but after a few rounds back and forth with her, Alex was able to give it back, and the family went on their way. Alex took a deep, shaky breath—the first one she'd consciously taken since the kid started choking—and a smile formed on her lips.

"Good work, kiddo," her mom said, patting her back. Alex looked at her, and her mom was smiling. "You're going to make a great paramedic when you graduate."

She looked proud, and it filled Alex with gratitude.

No matter how many times she'd had to argued for her decision to enroll at Evanston instead of going back to the University of Illinois, she knew that she'd made the right decision. Now her mom understood it, too.

Alex let out a sigh and said, "Thanks. I was about to suggest we go to the food court to get our dinner, but now maybe your appetite is spoiled?"

"Nope, I'm starving," her mom answered. "I *will* pass on the soft pretzels, though."

Alex laughed, and then in a more somber tone she said, "I'm sorry I threw away the television."

"It needed to be done," her mom replied. "We don't need it anymore."

TWENTY-SEVEN

Megan and Chloe were walking to class on the last day before Thanksgiving break. Chloe was talking about her research assignment and her excitement over the upcoming module, which would be on a new subject after the break. That explained why Ivy liked her so much as a study partner, because aside from throwing shade at her competitors, Megan had never heard Ivy utter a single thing that wasn't school-related.

For her part, Megan was thinking about her recent conversation with Alex, and wondering why she didn't have the guts to just apologize and tell her that she wanted to be with her. Megan hadn't stopped thinking about Alex since the night she kissed Chloe and messed it all up, and yet she couldn't bring herself to take the necessary leap of faith... if Alex would even be up for something like that after how she treated her.

When Megan and Chloe got to the lecture hall, the room was already nearly full so they found seats toward the back. Dr. Morrow had brought in a guest speaker, and Ivy was sitting front and center with her pen already poised over her notebook. Megan rolled her eyes and slumped into her seat while Chloe sat arrow-straight and alert beside her.

"Good morning, everyone," Dr. Morrow said as she approached the podium at the front of the room. "Today I've got a special treat in store for you, a little extra motivation to get you through the upcoming holiday break. If you please, join me in welcoming Dr. Lily Thomas, our guest speaker for the morning session."

The room broke into polite applause, and a woman sitting in the front row stood up and approached the podium. She was tall and remarkably pretty, with ebony skin and a hundred-watt smile that Megan could tell was friendly and genuine from all the way at the back of the room. She put her hands on either side of the lectern and said into the microphone, "Hello, I'm Dr. Thomas. Thank you for having me."

Her voice boomed into the room and a few people winced while she laughed, took a step back, and said, "Sorry about that. I'm not used to being amplified."

Megan could hear Ivy laughing from the front row. *Suck up.* Dr. Morrow made a quick adjustment to the microphone and then sat down in an open seat in the front row. She was just one chair away from Ivy, and that was probably making her day. Dr. Thomas continued, at a safe distance from the microphone this time.

"I'm a third-year resident in the pediatric department at Lakeside Hospital, and Dr. Morrow invited me here to talk to you all about the philosophy behind the phrase, *first do no harm,*" she said. "Who can tell me where that saying comes from?"

Ivy straightened up and shot her hand into the air, answering before Dr. Thomas could even finish pointing at her. "It's from the Latin *primum non nocere.*"

"Excellent," Dr. Thomas said. "It's something that we hear a lot in medicine, and we generally understand that it means our first obligation to our patients is to avoid medical intervention that will do more harm than good. Seems like a fine principle to live by, right?"

She paused, and a round of nods and murmurs of assent went through the room.

"It is," she said. "It is. Except when you let it paralyze you. All of you are at the half-way point of your medical school training, and your interactions with patients are going to become more frequent and more hands-on very soon. A lot of the time, medical students will get a case of the yips at this point in their careers, where they feel like they have a whole lot of knowledge but very little practical experience. Now that it's time to work on real patients, they find that they are afraid to do harm, to screw something up, to fail. *So they do nothing.*"

Megan sat up a little straighter in her chair. *Yeah,* she thought. That was exactly what she had been trying to do with Alex—avoid leaving her worse than when she met her. And she failed miserably.

"Let me tell you all a story from my childhood," Dr. Thomas said. "It's going to sound like a tangent, but I promise you'll start to see where I'm going with it soon.

To set the scene, I was eight years old, with two older brothers who never wanted anything to do with me because they were teenagers and I was an annoying little sister. My family went camping one weekend when I was in the second grade, and without their friends around, my brothers had to resort to playing with little old me."

A few people laughed, and Megan smiled. It was a feeling she could relate to—she never wanted anything to do with her younger brother Finn when she was a kid, and he was always so grateful when she'd throw him a bone now and then and act like he wasn't an annoying little twerp.

"My parents had just finished setting up the tents and building the fire to cook dinner," Dr. Thomas said. "They went down to the lake not far from the campsite to catch a few fish, and my brothers and I were playing the most pathetic game of football ever. Okay, I guess you couldn't call it that. They were tossing the ball back and forth to each other and I was running around like a lunatic, demanding loudly that they pass me the ball."

She paused as a murmur of laughter rippled through the room, and then went on with a little more weight in her voice.

"I finally convinced them to pass me the ball. My brother, Jace, told me to go long and I did. I was so excited to finally get my chance at catching the ball that I didn't hear them both screaming at me to look out and I went so long that I stepped right into the campfire," she said. "I sustained second degree burns over fourteen percent of my body and I spent almost a month in the hospital."

There were a few awed sounds throughout the room, and Dr. Thomas let this sink in for a moment. Then she stepped out from behind the podium, staying close enough to use the microphone. She pointed at her right leg.

"As you can see, I lived to tell the tale, and I have full function of the affected area," she said. "Not all burn patients are so lucky, and I know for a fact that the reason I'm telling you this story and not a more tragic one is because of the bravery and good instincts of my medical team. When I arrived at the hospital, I was unconscious and it didn't look good. The lead doctor on my team said that the best course of action would be to debride, cover, and stabilize before making any further treatment decisions, but there was this one spunky resident who thought I could handle a more aggressive treatment.

"He argued for early surgical intervention to remove the dead tissue, which would also reduce the risk of infection and lead to far better functional and aesthetic outcomes," she said. "He had to fight for that, and justify his recommendation, and convince every member of that team—along with my terrified parents—that what he wanted would do more good than harm. He won that battle, and I won the full use of my leg."

Dr. Thomas stepped back behind the podium and continued.

"I'm not asking you to know everything, or to be completely confident in every one of your decisions right out of the gate. It would be dangerous if you were," she said. "What I *am* asking you to do is remember what you've learned here and never forget that there are worlds of knowledge that you don't yet have, and that you may never have. Be aware of what you don't know, which is the hard part, and then rely on your instinct and training to know when to take a risk. You have a support system, so don't ever be afraid to lean on it, and don't let yourself be paralyzed. Do no harm, but fight for what you believe is right."

MEGAN WALKED home from class that day with Dr. Thomas's words resonating in her mind. They kept contrasting with the last conversation she'd had with Alex, and Megan finally realized that what Dr. Thomas had said—and what Chloe had been saying for weeks— was true. She had become paralyzed by the fear of falling for Alex because she was afraid to lose her. But what had that fear done for her besides throw a cherry bomb into their relationship and hurt everyone involved?

She went back to the apartment and watched Chloe pack for her bus ride home for the long Thanksgiving weekend, and she wondered if it was too late to win Alex back. She hoped not, and she was ready to try again, just as soon as she had the apartment to herself.

TWENTY-EIGHT

Alex went to her last class before the break, and then she and Sarah went to the college library together to schedule their certification exams. They'd have just a few more weeks of class after Thanksgiving, and then the program would be complete and it would be time to take the test. Alex thought that would probably be enough time to get Megan out of her head, after she'd definitively told Alex that she had no room or desire for dating. Five or six weeks to forget about her and focus on studying, and then there would be a small graduation ceremony and Alex would be an Emergency Medical Technician, trained and ready to work.

That was why, a few days before Thanksgiving, she was confused and a little dismayed to find her phone ringing, the name on the screen being Megan's. Alex pushed aside the notes she'd spread across her desk and looked at her phone for a minute, wondering if she should even answer. In the end, though, it was impossible not to.

"Megan?" she asked in lieu of *hello*.

"Hey," Megan answered. "Am I calling at a bad time?"

"No," Alex said. "I'm just studying for my certification exam."

"Already?"

"It's not until January, but I wanted to get a head start," Alex said. She struggled to find the right words to ask Megan the reason for her call. *Why are you calling me?* seemed too harsh, but the suspense was killing her so she settled on, "What's up?"

"Not much," Megan said. "My roommate just went home for Thanksgiving, and I was thinking about you."

She sounded nervous, a rare trait for Megan.

"You were?" Alex asked.

"Yeah," Megan said. "Umm, how have you been?"

"Fine," Alex said, her tone guarded. "School's almost over already, and my mom's finally starting to put in some job applications. We're doing good."

"Oh, that's good," Megan said. "Good for her."

Then with a little hesitation, Alex asked, "What about you?"

Megan didn't answer right away. The line remained quiet so long that Alex had to check to make sure they were still connected, and then finally she said, "I've been such an idiot. I can't stop thinking about you and how I probably destroyed any hope of being with such an amazing person by just being a complete tool. Alex, I'm so sorry and I don't know why it took me so long to realize that I was repeating history. I guess I'm a bit dense."

"Yeah, you are," Alex said, smiling sympathetically even though Megan couldn't see it.

"I was wondering," Megan said, "if you would meet me sometime when you're free so that I can give you a proper apology."

"I'm free now," Alex blurted, much faster than she'd intended to. Was she really going to let Megan off the hook this quickly? Her heart was screaming for her to do just that, but she knew it couldn't be so easy. She would meet Megan and see what she had to say, but it had better be good.

"Okay," Megan said, her spirits lifted. "We could meet at the coffee shop, or the diner, and hopefully get a private booth where people won't be listening to our conversation. Or you could come over to my apartment."

She said this last part tentatively, and Alex wondered if it was Megan's intention all along—her roommate wasn't home and she was feeling lonely, so she figured she'd see if Alex was game. *That* was not going to happen, but on the other hand, Alex wasn't in the mood for coffee or diner food. She just wanted to talk, so she agreed, telling herself that she'd be out the door at the first sign that Megan had ulterior motives.

"I'll come over," she said. "Just give me a few minutes."

"Okay," Megan said. "Thank you."

Alex hung up, put on her coat, and then peeked into the living room. Her mother was sitting on the couch with her computer in her lap, typing furiously.

"What are you doing, ma?" she asked as she went over to the front door to pull on her boots.

"I decided to sell some of my Home Shopping Network stash on eBay," she said. "Most of it has never been out of the box, and I was thinking it might be nice to convert the garage into a little home gym. What do you think?"

"I like it," Alex said. She thought that her dad would have liked it, too. "Hey, I'm going out for a little while, okay?"

"Okay, baby. Where are you headed?"

"Megan just called me," Alex said. "She wants to talk."

Her mom looked up from the computer and gave her a knowing look, then said, "Good luck."

THE TWENTY-MINUTE DRIVE across town was one of the longest of Alex's life. Her pulse was racing the whole time, and big white snowflakes were falling relentlessly across her windshield. She tried to guess what Megan would have to say when she got there, or what she would say in return, but after everything they'd gone through and done to each other in the past couple of months, Alex really had no clue.

When she parked on the street in front of Megan's apartment building, she was surprised to see Megan standing on the front stoop, her hands in her parka and her shoulders hunched up close to her ears like she had been there a while.

Alex got out of her car and walked up the sidewalk, asking, "What are you doing out here?"

"It was the least I could do after you drove all the way over here," she said. "Plus you've only been here once, so I wasn't sure you remembered which apartment was mine."

Alex came to a stop a few feet from Megan and her heart was pounding out a drum solo in her chest. What on earth was she doing here, and why did those giant, fluffy snowflakes have to fall on Megan's fiery hair in such a magical way? The streetlight lit up the snow like fairy dust and she didn't think it was possible for Megan's emerald eyes to be any more beautiful. Alex missed that sight tremendously.

"So," Megan said, "do you want to come in?"

"Sure," Alex said, a shiver running through her, but she didn't move. "Why did you call me tonight?"

"I told you," Megan said. "I realized how stupid I've been and I wanted to see if there's any possibility that I can make it up to you, even though you have every right to hate me."

"I don't hate you," Alex said. "I'm frustrated that you were more interested in holding onto that lie you tell yourself about hurting people you love than actually giving love a try, but I don't hate you."

"Well, that's a start," Megan said with a small smile. She held out her hand and said, "Come on."

"I'm not here for anything other than an apology," Alex said, trying to convince herself of that fact.

"Of course," Megan said, furrowing her brow as if any other motive had never occurred to her. If she was lying, she was damn good at it. Alex didn't take her hand, but she did follow her into the apartment building.

TWENTY-NINE

Megan led Alex up the stairwell to her apartment. She took Alex's coat and hung it on the hook by the wall, added her own, and then motioned Alex toward the couch in the living room while she went to the kitchen and asked, "Do you want some coffee?"

She'd spent most of the time waiting for Alex to arrive pacing the living room, wondering if it was too late for apologies, but she had managed to brew a pot of coffee. It was currently filling the apartment with its caramel aroma, and Alex nodded.

"Sure," she said, sitting down and waiting for Megan to join her.

Things were tense, and Megan wasn't quite sure how to proceed. She'd thought a lot about what it would be like to see Alex again, and she knew all of the things she should say, but actually getting them out of her mouth was another thing all together. Now that Alex was here in her apartment, Megan's words were gone along with her courage. She poured two cups of coffee and tried to muster the right words as she came over and handed one of them to Alex.

"You take it black, right?"

"Yep," Alex said, glancing into Megan's cup. "And you take yours with so much cream and sugar it can hardly be considered coffee."

Megan smiled and then hung her head in mock shame. That was more like the dynamic that she missed so much when she was with Alex, and she wanted very badly to get back there. She took a quick sip, and then began.

"I'm sorry that I reacted the way I did," she said. "I haven't allowed someone to get close to me in a very long time, and the way you make me feel scares the hell out of me. I never pursued Chloe, and I wasn't expecting that kiss, but when it happened I think subconsciously I decided it would be an easy way to push you away and protect my own heart. Then when you caught us, I reacted coldly and cruelly. I thought it would be easier for us both to just sever ties so that I couldn't hurt you further."

"You did hurt me," Alex said. "Seeing you kiss that girl was very painful, and having you look at me as if I was the one who shouldn't be there was even worse. But you hurt me the most when you refused to acknowledge the fact that we had something special. We weren't just fooling around—we barely did that. You helped me get past the most difficult time of my life, and I know that I could help you get over your own issues if you'd just let me in."

"Do you still want that?" Megan asked hopefully. She was almost afraid to hear the answer, because now was when she'd find out whether she'd waited too long, or screwed up too badly.

"That depends on you," Alex said. "Are you ready to stop running?"

"Yes," Megan said. "The reality of not being with you is far worse than the risk of losing you at some point in the future, and I pray that I haven't lost you already. I know I have a long way to go in making it up to you, but if you'll let me, I'd like to get started. I want to be with you, and I promise that I'll never push you away again."

"And I'm not going to let you push me away just because you're afraid," Alex said, putting her mug down and taking Megan's hand. "You think you're the only one who's scared?"

Megan laughed, relief washing over her. A single tear escaped Megan's eye, but it only made it halfway down her cheek before Alex swiped it away for her.

"Are you sure you want to be with someone as broken as me?" Megan asked, trepidation rising suddenly in her throat. She wanted to make sure Alex knew what she was in for.

"You're not broken," Alex said. "Or if you are, it's not worse than me. Have you ever heard of *kintsugi*?"

"Heard of what now?" Megan asked.

"*Kintsugi,* the Japanese art of repairing broken pottery,"

Alex explained. "I learned about it in my art classes. Potters will repair broken pieces with gold or silver dust that improves the aesthetic quality of the new version of the piece. The Japanese consider it to be more beautiful *because* it was broken. Megan, you're stronger than you think."

"I'm not a pot," she said. "I've been like this a long time and it's going to take more than a little gold dust to fix me."

"I don't care if I have to spent the rest of my life figuring out how your pieces fit together," Alex said. "I want to be with you, and as long as I know you're in this with me, I'm never going to stop fighting for you."

"I am," Megan breathed, and it felt like a weight being lifted from her chest. "I'm in this, completely."

Then Alex put her hand on Megan's cheek and drew their lips together. Satisfaction bloomed throughout Megan's entire body—this was exactly what she'd been waiting for, and what she hadn't dared hope for. It felt like coming home. Alex's lips were warm against her skin, her breath tasting faintly of the coffee that they'd barely drank.

Megan slid her arms around Alex's waist and pulled her into a tight hug, enjoying the curves of her body against her. Alex closed her eyes and let out a low moan, and Megan tentatively slid her tongue into Alex's mouth. Alex's tongue met hers, and the sensation sent another shiver of desire through her. She moved slowly, laying Alex back against the plush cushions of the couch and keeping her close, enjoying the warmth of her body that had built inside of her heavy coat.

She slid her hands very slowly up Alex's sides, enjoying every curve and every small moan that she elicited. She skimmed her fingers beneath Alex's sweater, nudging the soft fabric up slowly inch by inch. When she had revealed Alex's light pink bra and the curve of her breasts beneath it, Megan brought her lips down to meet Alex's skin. She kissed a trail down her chest, hooking one finger gently beneath the cup of Alex's bra and pulling it down so that her mouth could find the soft flesh there, kissing and licking her in slow circles.

Alex arched her back and pressed her body into Megan when she closed her mouth over her nipple, the feeling of her hips connecting with Megan's sending desire through her. Megan's body awakened and she had to resist the urge to squeeze, to bite, to press herself urgently against Alex. She'd missed her so much.

They had all night, and she intended to make the moment last. It was the least she could do after the leap of faith Alex had taken to come here tonight, and the promise she had made. *I'm never going to stop fighting for you.* Megan murmured the sentiment into Alex's skin, prompting her to raise her head and ask, "What?"

"I said I will never stop fighting for you, either," Megan said. "You're perfect for me."

Alex smiled, her eyes lighting up, and then Megan dipped her head back down to meet Alex's chest. She inched her way down to the other end of the couch, kissing Alex's stomach as she went. Megan slid her hands down Alex's hips, enjoying the rough denim of her jeans against her palms. She unbuttoned them, kissing the skin that peaked out over her waistband as she did it. Alex moved her hips forward, seeking contact with Megan, and Megan pulled her pants down over her hips.

Megan inhaled the scent of her, groaning, and she never wanted to leave Alex's side again. She wanted to wrap her arms around her waist and hold her tight. Instead, she used her lips and tongue to tease her, kissing and licking the skin of her stomach, then her thighs, then the ridges of her hips until Alex let out a frustrated sigh and raised her hips to meet Megan's mouth.

Finally, she slipped her fingers beneath the waistband of Alex's panties and slid them slowly down her thighs. Megan kissed her pubic bone and then she breathed hotly against Alex's skin, causing a minor quake to originate in her hips and echo outward to the rest of her body. Alex spread her thighs a little farther apart and wrapped her legs around Megan, and Megan lowered her lips to meet Alex's trembling, aching flesh.

She reached one hand up Alex's bare stomach and found the soft flesh of her breast, kneading and squeezing her and enjoying the way that Alex's hips began to take on a life of their own, moving beneath Megan's touch.

Megan took her time, paying attention to every part of Alex's body and enjoying the increasing urgency of her responses. With every lick, suck and caress, Alex's breathing became a little more labored, a little faster, until she lost control of herself. Her hips moved and reached and craved Megan all of their own accord until she had to put her arms around Alex's thighs to hold her still.

Alex let out a moan as her body shook and her belly trembled and Megan teased a long, intense orgasm out of her. Alex tangled her fingers into Megan's hair as she kept moving her tongue, closing her lips around Alex until finally she drew her thighs together against Megan's head, left out one last whimper, and went limp on the couch.

Megan crawled up to meet her and she wrapped her arms around Alex, holding her tight and protecting her against any draft that might chill her.

THIRTY

Alex took a moment to catch her breath, this orgasm even more intense than the ones Megan had given her the first time they were together. She threw her arms around Megan and they laid together in a tight embrace for a few minutes until her energy returned.

She nuzzled into Megan's body, her face finding the crook of her neck, and she kissed her as Megan asked, "What are you doing?"

Alex slid her hands down Megan's stomach and beneath the waistband of her leggings, finding wetness and desire there. She murmured into Megan's neck, "What does it feel like?"

"It feels great," Megan said, her hand going down and covering Alex's as she pressed her palm more firmly against her and her hips answered back.

The move sent a second shiver of desire through Alex and she felt hungry, like she could spend the whole night making up for the year in which she'd felt nothing at all. She was ready for Megan's touch again already

She slid one finger through the wetness between Megan's thighs and parted her legs to allow their hips to join. Megan rolled her hips in rhythmic movements against Alex's palm and she sat up, climbing on top of Megan to kiss her, touch her, and take control.

She slipped her tongue into Megan's mouth, tasting herself on Megan's lips as her hand glided back and forth between her legs. Megan moaned and put her hands on Alex's hips, squeezing the ample flesh there and increasing her desire as Alex began to move her hips to match the rhythm of Megan's own.

They were moaning and moving together, their breathing intensified, and Alex yanked Megan's leggings down over her hips, taking her panties with them in one motion. She slid off the couch, coming to her knees and pulling Megan into a sitting position as she desperately sought her out. Alex pushed Megan's knees wide and yanked her hips to the edge of the couch cushion, and then she brought her head down to meet her trembling flesh.

She slid one finger inside of her and Megan put her hand on Alex's head, her fingers winding into her hair as she gave in to the sensations Alex was causing, allowing her body to tip over into a climax that left her shaking and bucking her hips against Alex's hand.

Then Megan reached for Alex, pulling her back onto the couch with a kiss. She grabbed a thick knitted blanket off the back of the couch and wrapped it around both of them, then snuggled into Alex with her arms wrapped around her waist to ward off the cold.

———

ALEX WOKE up early the next morning, her arms wrapped contently around Megan. The knit blanket they'd fallen asleep under was warm, and the apartment felt peaceful and comfortable.

Megan began to stir beneath her, her breath warm against Alex's skin, and when she roused from her sleep she looked up at her with those big emerald eyes and smiled. It was a beautiful sight.

"Good morning," she said.

"Morning," Alex answered, giving Megan a tight squeeze and then releasing her to throw her arms overhead in a big stretch. She felt a little stiff from spending the night on the couch, but it was well worth it. "What time do you think it is?"

"Early," Megan said. "It's not quite daylight outside yet."

She kissed Alex, gathering her up in her arms as she did it, and then she bent over the edge of the couch to find her sweater. She pulled it on, along with her panties, and got up. Alex whimpered at her absence, suddenly feeling a little bit cold, so she pulled the blanket tighter around her. Megan took their coffee mugs to the sink and dumped out the icy remnants, and while she was loading the mugs into the dishwasher, Alex wrapped the blanket around her and got up, too.

She went over to the window and looked outside, where the street was completely blanketed in fluffy white snow. Her car had at least two inches on it and she wondered if her mother was up yet. She hadn't expected to stay, and she hadn't spent the night away from home since her father died. She felt a little guilty about it, especially since her mom didn't even have a television to keep her company anymore.

"I should go," she said as Megan came over to join her.

"Really?" Megan asked sadly.

"Yeah," Alex said. "My mom's probably worried about me."

"Okay," Megan said, but she wrapped her arms around Alex, sliding her hands beneath the layers of the blanket to connect with her. Then she asked, "What do the two of you do for Thanksgiving?"

"I don't know," Alex said. "Last year we weren't in the mood to celebrate so we just ate frozen lasagna and my mom bought a cordless vacuum that she never took out of the box."

Megan looked saddened by this, and Alex realized how pathetic it sounded. She laughed and tried to lighten the mood.

"That was only a few months after my dad died," she said. "This year we can probably do better for ourselves. I was thinking of making my dad's favorite cookies—they're kind of involved, so that should keep us busy for a while."

"Okay, I just had a crazy idea," Megan said. "Feel free to turn it down, but why don't you and your mom come over to my family's house for Thanksgiving dinner instead? You could bring the cookie ingredients with you and we can all make them together."

"I wouldn't want to impose," Alex said.

"You're not imposing," Megan insisted. "I don't ever want you to leave my side again... If you and your mom are up for it, I would love to have you there."

"I think I can convince her," Alex said. "Are you sure it's not an imposition? Thanksgiving is only a couple days away and I wouldn't want your mom to have to feed two more mouths on such short notice."

"Are you kidding?" Megan asked. "You don't know my mom yet, but when you meet her you'll see that having two more mouths to feed is going to be the best thing about her Thanksgiving holiday."

"Okay," Alex said, smiling at Megan. "Let's do it."

"Awesome," Megan said with a grin. "So can you stay a little longer? I finally don't have homework to catch up on, and I want nothing more than to keep you in my arms for as long as possible."

Alex broke into a wide grin and kissed her, then said, "Yeah, I can stay. I just need to text my mom to let her know I'm not dead."

She went over to her coat on the hook by the door and fished her phone out of her pocket, and when she was done, Megan came over and wrapped her arms around her again, kissing the crook of her neck. She said, "I think I'm going to take a quick shower."

"Okay," Alex said, but when Megan unwrapped her

arms, she took Alex by the hand and started to pull her down the hall. She asked, curious, "What?"

"Come on," Megan said with a wink. "I said I didn't want to let you go."

"Okay," Alex answered, catching on. She let Megan lead her down the hall and into the bathroom. Alex let out a happy laugh as Megan threw the blanket off Alex's shoulders and tossed it into the hallway before she swung the bathroom door shut.

THE END

Want to know what's next for Megan and Alex? Subscribe to my newsletter at http://eepurl.com/cCBjff for exclusive access to bonus chapters and deleted scenes.

A NOTE FROM THE AUTHOR

Thanks for reading *The Origins of Heartbreak,* the first novel in my medical romance series – I hope you enjoyed it!

If you did, please consider leaving a review on Amazon or Goodreads – they make a big difference in the success of a new book, and reviews help more readers find new LGBT authors like me.

Thanks again for reading, and I hope to hear from you soon!

With love,
Cara

ALSO BY CARA MALONE

It's Christmas at the Emerald Mountain Ski Resort, and Joy is looking for her next vacation girlfriend to keep her company through the snowy nights. Carmen seems like just the girl for the task, if not for her bah humbug attitude and Scrooge-like family. Can Joy remind them all of the spirit of the season in time to meet Carmen beneath the mistletoe?

Visit www.caramalonebooks.com/
for a complete list of books by Cara Malone.

J oy Valentine could feel tears forming in the back of her throat. She was not the kind of girl who gave in to that urge to cry, though, so she swallowed hard and pressed her lips into a thin smile.

"You're going to make a great dad," she said, pulling her best friend, Ross, into a tight hug.

When she released him, he looked at her with cynicism and said, "Really? What evidence have you ever seen to support that claim?"

"I don't know," Joy said, punching his shoulder. "It just seemed like something people say in situations like this."

"Well, I appreciate the platitude," Ross said, "but I'm about to drive across the country to become a parent with a girl I hooked up with a few times while doing illicit drugs. I don't know what part of that equation you think spells 'Dad of the Year'."

They both laughed – there was nothing else they

could do, and it seemed to help cut the tension between them. Ross was driving to Ohio tonight in his old, rusted out Jeep, and neither one of them knew what to expect beyond that vague plan. Joy had a feeling in her gut that he was leaving her forever, and she'd been doing her best to ignore it for the past few weeks ever since he told her about the plan. Ross had been her best friend since elementary school, and he was one of the few people who stuck around Emerald Hill after graduation, and now there was a very real possibility that he was leaving her forever.

He picked up the oversized duffel bag that had been laying at his feet in the middle of their living room, and Joy thought fleetingly that at least the majority of his stuff was still strewn about their shared apartment. If he stayed in Ohio to be with the baby, at least he'd have to come back one last time and pack up his stuff.

Joy let out a shaky breath, steeling herself for the quickly approaching moment when she'd have to watch him drive away, and Ross caught her apprehensive look.

"I'll be back in a couple of weeks," he said.

"Yeah, right," Joy responded.

Ross slung the duffel bag over his shoulder and she followed him outside, watching as he heaved it into the back of the Jeep and then came back around to the driver's door where she stood waiting for him. He asked, "You're going to keep me posted on the Emerald Hill gossip, right?"

"Totally," Joy said. "All the ridiculous room service

requests and rich people temper tantrums you could want."

This season at the ski resort wouldn't be the same without him, and even if he really did come back in a few weeks, Joy would have to get through the Christmas rush without Ross. It was already December sixteenth, and Allison hadn't even gone into labor yet. With any luck, Ross would end up with a Christmas baby.

"Don't forget about the single-serving girlfriend," Ross reminded her. "I want all those juicy details, too."

Joy rolled her eyes, wondering if she'd have the energy for a holiday fling this year. The single-serving lover had been a tradition that she and Ross began years ago, when they first started working at the resort together after high school, and once upon a time, Allison herself had been the flavor of the month. Now she was carrying Ross's child and ready to pop at any moment, so clearly that hadn't turned out as intended.

"I don't know," she said. "Maybe I'll take a powder this year and just focus on work. Johnson says I've got management potential if I buckle down."

"Who wants that?" Ross asked incredulously. "Get out there and find the hottest girl on the slopes to spend the holiday with, and then let me live vicariously through you. I'm probably going to be up to my elbows in dirty diapers while you're out here, so don't squander the opportunity."

"Yes, sir," Joy said, still not fully convinced. Ross climbed into the Jeep and she said, "Let me know when you get there, and send me pictures when the baby comes."

"Will do," he said, and then he threw the truck into reverse and pulled out onto the snowy road that would take him to meet his child. Joy stood in the parking lot in front of their apartment building for a few minutes, watching the Jeep recede into the distance and clenching her hands into fists to keep herself from crying.

CARMEN CRANE WAS SITTING in one corner of a big, velvet-lined booth at The Palms. It was a rare Saturday night that didn't find her there with her friends, and an early-morning flight to Colorado certainly wouldn't stop her from joining them.

"Why *Colorado*?" Carmen's best friend, Brigid, asked, her upper lip curling in disgust as she said the name of her destination. She couldn't believe that anyone would actually *choose* snow at Christmas, and neither could Carmen. Brigid asked plaintively, "What's wrong with Cancun?"

Carmen sighed and took a liberal sip from her martini glass. She'd had to send one of the guys over to the bar to get it for her, and it was irritating that she was still several years away from being able to order her own drinks. They spent enough time at The Palms and rang up big enough tabs, so she thought the bartenders should look the other way and stamp her hand.

"Not a damned thing," she said. Colorado had been

her father's idea, some half-baked idea to take a trip down memory lane or something like that, even though the closest the Cranes had ever gotten to a ski vacation in Carmen's childhood was sledding down the icy hills in her run-down hometown in Massachusetts.

This year, Carmen and her family were at the mercy of her father, doomed to freeze their buns off on a mountainside all in the name of Christmas cheer, or something stupid like that. Meanwhile, all of Carmen's friends would be sunning themselves on the beach and day-drinking themselves into oblivion like they did every year. She knew it was too late to get out of the trip, but she could at least enjoy one last night with her friends before they all left for their objectively superior vacation.

"Honestly," said one of the guys, Bentley, as he crashed into the booth beside them and squished Brigid into Carmen, nearly causing her to spill her drink all over her lap. She hissed at him – *Watch it!* – but he paid her no attention as he just kept talking. "Everyone knows you're not an outdoor kind of girl. What the hell are you going to do for ten days at a ski resort?"

"Yeah," Brigid said, tittering and batting her eyelashes transparently at Bentley in a way that never failed to make Carmen's stomach turn over. They'd hooked up so many times, ever since sophomore year of high school, and yet it didn't seem like Brigid was ever going to realize he was using her. She sure as hell was going to keep trying to impress him, though. Carmen rolled her eyes as Brigid added to his quip, "She's probably going to go all Jack Torrence in *The Shining* after the first day."

"Heeeere's Johnny!" Bentley screeched, and Carmen had a nearly uncontrollable urge to kick him in the face with her five-inch Louboutins.

Rather than allowing herself the space to wonder why exactly she called these people her friends, she tipped her glass back and emptied it, then shot back her reply. "Bentley, you don't know anything about me. I'm going to dominate those ski hills."

"I think they're called slopes," he said, smirking while Brigid laughed and fell exaggeratedly onto him in her hysterics. She really wasn't a bad friend when Bentley wasn't around, but those moments had become fewer and far between in the last few years until it seemed like Carmen couldn't get a moment alone with her best friend, and Brigid had slowly turned into some unrecognizable, giggling and vapid shell of herself.

"Yeah, slopes. Whatever," Carmen said. "While you're in Cancun, getting smashed and taking the same bare-chested glamor selfies you always take, I'm going to be having an actual unique vacation experience."

"Sure, if you want to call sitting in your room, looking at my Cancun photos on Instagram unique," Bentley said. "I bet that'll be a vacation like no other."

Brigid laughed again, and it was starting to really get on Carmen's nerves. When the hell had this cocky jerk wormed his way into their social group so completely that it would require a surgeon to extract Brigid from his ass? She leaned over the back of the booth, waving one of their friends off the dance floor and calling to him, "Hey, Dawson, could you be a pal and get me another martini? Dirty, with three – no, four – olives."

It was going to take more than that to make watching Brigid and Bentley suck face for the rest of the night tolerable, and Carmen could already tell that was the direction they were heading. While Dawson went over to the bar on her behalf, she flopped back down in the booth and said, "How about a little wager?"

"What do you have in mind?" Bentley asked, perking up immediately. He was always a sucker for bets, and this time Carmen was only too happy to play into this vice if it meant getting him off her back for a little while.

"I'll take a selfie on the mountain, in my skis, having a way better time than you," she said. "And in exchange, you'll leave me and Brigid alone for the entire month of January and find your own crew to hang out with."

"But-" Brigid began to object, but Bentley was too involved in the bet to allow her to finish her thought.

"And if you chicken out and never leave the lodge?" he asked.

"Then *I'll* leave you to suck each other's faces off in this booth by yourselves for the entire year," Carmen said. Maybe it was the martinis talking – she was already on her fourth, and saw her fifth one making its way to her across the crowded room – but she really didn't think skiing would be all that hard. At the very least, she could pay a ski instructor to take her to the top of the mountain and hold the camera while she faked a few sick moves, enough to get Bentley out of her life for a little while.

"Deal," he said, reaching across Brigid's lap to shake Carmen's hand. "But I'm pretty sure if you try it you're going to be coming back to New York in traction."

"We'll see," Carmen said, letting go of his hand and conspicuously wiping the moisture from his palm onto the booth.

Then she got up and squeezed past them, meeting Dawson on the edge of the dance floor and taking the martini from him. There were only six more hours before her flight to Emerald Hill and she knew that the responsible thing would be to stop drinking and go home and get a little sleep. But Carmen hadn't done anything intentionally responsible in at least a dozen years, and she didn't intend to start now. She downed the martini in a few quick gulps, set down the empty glass, and then joined Dawson on the dance floor.

She'd be hung over and regretting this decision later, when her mother was keeping the flight attendants busy and her twin sisters, Spencer and Sidney, were screeching and playing whatever stupid video game was trending in the seats behind her, but for now, there was dancing to be done.

Continue reading...

23160002R00136

Printed in Poland
by Amazon Fulfillment
Poland Sp. z o.o., Wrocław